To Nancy,

To my dear friend

Love

Kelly

Wild Child

(A Coming of Age Memoir)

By

Isadora Kelly

Table OF Contents

Dedication..v

Acknowledgments...vi

Introduction...vii

Chapter 1: Losing My Virginity...................................1

Chapter 2: James Rector 10

Chapter 3: Last of the Canadian Lovers....................26

Chapter 4: Terry Cooper 40

Chapter 5: Kyle Singer 50

Chapter 6: Eric Wilson & Ron Franco.......................60

Chapter 7: Blowjobs & Definitions 78

Chapter 8: Lilly & Modeling 86

Chapter 9: Desmond Perreira 100

Chapter 10: Phil's Friend Heath 116

Chapter 11: Phil Klang...124

Chapter 12: Jeff Dawson..134

Chapter 13: Darby Vanderbilt 144

Chapter 14: Ben Baker 156

Chapter 15: Fun Times with Shelly & Rosemary 163

Chapter 16: An Interlude - Neil Dennis 170

Chapter 17: High School Antics 177

Chapter 18: Off to College...................................187

Chapter 19: Michelle Mustain 199

Chapter 20: Lust 206

Chapter 21: Variety 213

Chapter 22: The Pearsons...................................219

Chapter 23: Surgeons...225

Chapter 24: Hellen & Erlich................................229

Chapter 25: Lincoln Center.................................237

Dedication

This book is dedicated to my parents, who were adamant that I could do anything a guy could do. They always encouraged me to try to do whatever I wanted.

Acknowledgments

First, I wish to thank the wonderful and generous lovers I have been blessed with, and without their attention and enthusiasm, I could not have written this book. Second, I want to thank my friends at Payne Equestrian, Doug and Jess Payne, who ride and train my two show jumpers, who they found. The horses they found are doing really well.

Introduction

This book covers the 60s and 70s. Oh, what a time it was! Where everything was permitted, and people didn't fall prey to jealousy, hatred, and all manner of dysfunction. Trust me; this is what really happened back in the day. It was a wild time, and contrary to popular opinion, we lived the best life imaginable. We were not drug addicts looking for the latest high.

No, on the contrary, for the first time in history, we became the masters of our own destinies. All the repression, conditioning, and principles went out the window. For us (and, of course, me), values didn't depend on moralizing or possessiveness. The only value we had was living life to the fullest potential, and boy, did we live.

You people may wonder why I wrote this book. Well, the simple answer is that I am a voracious reader and read two to four books a week. This is my usual routine, and I have been following it for as long as I can remember. However, till now, I have never come across a single book that accurately depicts the 60s and 70s and, more importantly, the sexual revolution. Trust me when I say this, the birth control pill was a HUGE invention. Many people fail to recognize the impact the pill and the sexual revolution had on society as a whole.

No longer were women at risk of getting knocked up in the heat of passion. Through the pill, women were free to pursue sex in the most open, flamboyant, and adventurous way. This tremendously affected women and changed the mores of society forever. In other words, the commonly-held expectations of women were no longer valid. Women were free to pursue their sexuality as and with whomever they pleased.

I can still recall magazines like *Cosmopolitan* writing articles about sexual techniques that were previously unheard of or considered taboo. These articles were immensely educational. There were also books I liked a lot, including *The Kama Sutra*, *The Joy of Sex*, and *The Happy Hooker*. Through these books, I (and probably many women) learned to enjoy sex just for the sake of it. Now, women were allowed to indulge and appreciate intimacy on another level.

This was my education, and I think I applied it well. I have vignettes that describe my lifestyle vividly during the 60s and 70s. I have close to 80 of them. Though, in this book, we are using just the ones that really apply and can turn into proper and detailed chapters. Yet, there are a number of short vignettes that I feel helped me in completing this book. These other vignettes will help you understand what I was going through and how I came to terms with some of the wild things I did.

Make no mistake—I was a wild child through and through. But I had lots of fun and gave immense pleasure to various people in my life. To this day, I have never read any book or personal account that accurately describes the lifestyle of the 1960s and 1970s. Granted, there are magazines like *Cosmopolitan* that have a lot of stuff about sex, and other books exist. But this is my story, and I have explained it in as much detail as I could. The sex is all about my lovers and me, and it's very graphic. So, don't buy this book if you are put off by explicit content. To sum it up, this book is a memoir of my many exploits. It contains graphic details of the encounters I had with several lovers.

Obviously, the names of my lovers will not be disclosed to protect their identities if they are still alive. I am sure they will recognize themselves once the book is published. Personally, I prefer older, more experienced lovers, although there are some notable exceptions. You will get more vivid details as you read on. Unfortunately, the big problem with having older lovers is that they don't last long…well, not that. I mean, they die too early. I have made contact with some of them, and they are all dying.

Yet still, the memories I had with them will live on. This book is nothing but the vignettes of my colorful life put together. It contains various chapters dedicated to my favorite lovers that are not long but which, for some reason, add something to the storyline. I hope you enjoy it. I've been working on it on and off for a considerable amount of time.

I lost my journals for a couple of years, and that put me way back because I recorded most of my sexual exploits in these journals as they happened. After eight years, I finally buckled down, found my journals, and began drafting this book. To tell you the truth, I've been rehearsing this book in my head for a long time, and I hope that it brings joy and excitement to your life.

I look forward to hearing just how my book has impacted your life. Please, don't be too shocked by it. I have shared my book with many of my friends and asked what they think of it. They told me that it brings back a lot of memories for them, especially their time during the 60s and 70s. Their responses greatly encouraged me, and I eagerly await the feedback I will receive on my many trysts and conquests.

I also revealed my stories to certain unaware friends, and they laughed hysterically at some of my antics. Stories such as how I learned to give blow jobs in a closet that I thought was a bedroom. He had a big door to a giant old closet that was probably meant for luggage. He was this young gym teacher. Don't worry; there is an entire chapter dedicated to him. It was because of him that I learned how to give blowjobs the right way.

It was rough, and I absolutely loved it. By the way, let me point out that I love giving blowjobs. But more on that later in the book.

To get you an idea of how good I am, let me share the letters I received from my lover. These letters are from my lawyer friend, who was one of the top lawyers in the state. He was also the person who made me realize how I was as a lover and person. To be honest, I would've never put my experiences and my impact into words if it wasn't for him. The first letter read:

"Issy is the epitome of intellect, levity, compassion, and understanding. Her love of life has brought her happiness through professional accomplishments. Her personal success in equestrian events and her love of gentlemen with a gentle but firm touch. Her warm embrace fills your heart as only a true friend can. Her stunning beauty is always present with a caring touch and warm eyes. Her inner strength matches her outer strength. Her intelligence allows for comfortable conversations with substance. Her unique combination of brains and beauty is unsurpassed.

She is the desire of men, the envy of women, and loved by both. She is the one and only Issy."

The second letter he wrote was for a dating website called "Tinder," and it is a description of me as a lover. It read:

"Issy is a strong force with a great libido. Her passionate kisses allow for a strong embrace to match her powerful orgasms. She makes me feel like a desired man with the world at my fingertips. She's a sensual, sexual, faithful lover who gives satisfaction every time. Her long, lovely body brings desire as she gracefully moves over you, bringing desire in those fortunate enough to share her bed."

Talking a bit about my career, back in the 1980s and 1990s, I started working after having spent a year riding foxhunters and training them. Unfortunately, I broke my leg. As a result, I couldn't do much and had no insurance. Seeing my situation, my mother, at Christmas, went on to put the New York Times employment section in front of my face and said, "You've gone to some of the best colleges and universities in America. Don't you think you should get a real job?"

To tell you the truth, I was actually at the point where I was willing to do it. Instead of riding other people's horses, I would be able to afford to have my own horse. So, I started interviewing. Eventually, I wrote a very creative resume, which my father's old business friends and Mr. Pearson said that they would vouch for me.

After a few interviews, I started to realize they asked the same questions and wanted the same answers. But luckily, I got a job with Hitler's illegitimate son, who was a dealer in the New York area. I actually do think he could have been Hitler's illegitimate son, even though it was kind of a joke. The reason being he was Austrian, about the right age, and a real bastard. I learned quite a bit from him, but he really concentrated on the laboratory microscope business.

As a result, I was free to finally give the people of New Jersey good service, honesty, and things they hadn't had before from the dealer I was with. I managed to triple his business in one year by just going around just doing safety checks on the microscope. There were rings on the pole that went up and down and straps that had to be replaced with Teflon straps that had become damaged. I did all of this. I repaired the microscopes; I designed the systems. I spent all my time in the OR with Video Systems. At this time, neurosurgeons and ophthalmologists were just trying to learn how to use surgical microscopes.

They hadn't been trained at med school or their early residencies. Thus, I had a lot I could teach them. Also, with the video, I could see what they were doing and then explain to them the benefit of setting up the microscope properly and adjusting their eyepieces, like on a binocular.

These were all basically binocular microscopes with parallel beam pathways, these binoculars were focused into infinity, which allowed us to split off multiple surgical views. We could do this through video or the most difficult 35mm photography or, most commonly, just on the microscope with me watching and telling them what they needed to know. I became very popular in my territory. As I was always there, I was ready to loan them equipment.

At the same time, I would come in for big cases. I would stay for the whole case of neurosurgery which could take 12 hours. They would have flown a baby from LA for Dr. Carmel to operate on. We would joke that if you could just take the head off the person, it would make using a microscope much more easy. Since they were huge microscopes that hung off the ceiling or for any demos, they'd be on a stand. We had a free-floating microscope called the "Contraves," which, when balanced properly, which I was a master at. If someone bought a system from me, I would write an instruction on how to balance it on all three different axes and a ball and socket that the scope was attached to.

The scope would free float up to 70 pounds of microscope to just free-floating whenever you release the triggers, which could be with your hands or actually your teeth. You could buy a switch and move the microscope if it was properly balanced. To tell the truth, I adored my business. However, there was one major obstacle I had to deal with, Hitler's illegitimate son. He was such a bastard that one day I straight up went to Zeiss and said, "I will not work for him any longer. You have to give me a different situation."

They were giving away a dealership in New York. Ideally, they should have given it to me, but I was a girl. They picked a guy who was in the surgical business selling instruments. Although he knew nothing about surgical microscopes and how to use them, design them, or put them together. On the contrary, he was more interested in selling surgical suites and his instruments.

He had to hire someone to put the microscopes together and fix them and all of that, which were things I had done already. However, we had a good deal. We split the profit on any sales commissions that I got from the systems that I would sell. Moreover, I sold several systems and made a lot of money.

Before long, the new dealer started to hassle me about how much money I was making. In my perspective, we had a deal, first of all, and secondly, he got 50% of anything I sold. The only option I had was to sell very profitably. Zeiss had a great competitor called Wild or Veld, spelled Wild. We called it the Wild microscope, which we found very funny.

They gave me a huge territory, and I could sell as much as I wanted. For the next ten years, I had my exclusive business with Wild and sold so many microscopes that I was number one in the country. This continued for many years with Wild, but my health was starting to fail me, and no one knew what it was.

Eventually, the HR people at Zeiss found out how sick I was and could only participate in certain situations, at meetings, etc. They told the head of the Zeiss Medical Division that I had to be grounded and work from my home office.

When I couldn't work, I luckily had a very advanced hobby of showing my own horses in what's called the amateur-owner hunter division. In this, you had to own the horse. You can't just put some pro on to ride it. They're the highest fences for amateurs in the hunter division. My horse had been the "Horse of the Year" in the national championship the year I started showing him and ended up in Florida in Palm Beach at the Wellington horse shows. I filled up my time with riding lessons and showing at different events; I was basically creating a new life for myself.

At the same time, my husband of 21 years (we're now divorced for a while now) built a house in the place called the "Ford Plantation." He fell in love with it. It was beautiful. I was able to put all my OCD qualities (Obsessive Compulsive

Disorder) into building this historically accurate house. The entire process took about two years.

I was basically the onsite architect. We had a fabulous architect up in New Jersey who now builds like $40 million houses in Greenwich, Connecticut. He was a third-generation classical architect. He designed a beautiful house, although I picked out every piece of molding and every wood plank and placed them. Every piece of marble tile. I was very hands-on, and it was a great experience. I have gorgeous pictures of the house, which are in this book.

Looking back, it was foolish of me, but I had very bad advice locally. What I want to say is that I made something of my life besides just being a wild child in the 60s and 70s. I have a great life. I spend six months of the year in Canada and five and three-quarter months in the Carolinas, in a wonderful little town. In fact, the town has been voted "The Best Small Town in the South" by various travel magazines. That's where I live now.

I hope you will enjoy this book as it brings back memories of your past and the joy of being young. Again, please don't buy this book if you're affected negatively by explicit sexual descriptions, in many of the chapters and the description of I don't know 16-20 lovers that are the top of the hit parade for me. I'll let you decide because some of these lovers are slightly disguised to protect the innocent. There's a little bit of what I would call a novel in this memoir that holds it all together. So, keep on reading and know firsthand what life was truly like for me.

Chapter 1:

Losing My Virginity

This will be a rather amusing and interesting chapter because the loss of my virginity didn't happen in the ideal circumstances. Generally, teenage girls have this idea regarding how their virginity will end. This idea tends to involve their prince charming swiping them off their feet, taking them to a scenic location, and making love to them under the stars, you know, like in romantic movies and novels. What's more, most girls want it to be the most memorable experience of their life.

Well, my experience was memorable, but not in a good way. There were no rainbows, horses, beautiful gardens, or prince charming. That's just a fantasy concocted by a lot of wishful thinking. It doesn't happen in real life, even though many teenagers believe otherwise. Being a teenager myself, I also held a somewhat similar notion about losing my virginity. I didn't believe in a prince charming, but

I did expect the event to be magical and beautiful. Boy, was I wrong!

Looking back, I lost my virginity, as you'd probably guess, at a party. It was during this time I took a keen interest in fashion and beauty and envisioned myself becoming a model. I had several pictures taken of me and was hoping to make a name for myself in the industry. Then, one day, I got wind of a party being hosted by none other than Richard Hardman.

Armed with a number of pictures, I decided to go to the party. One of my three friends, Carol, was invited to a party on Bernardsville Mountain near our barn, where we rode horses. Carol had a huge crush on this guy Billy. I had brought my modeling pictures, and we showed them to various people at the party, and they couldn't even believe it was me.

As soon as they saw my pictures, people said things like, "This is you? Really is that you? God, you look absolutely stunning. You're really photogenic. You should start seeing agents by now."

I was deeply flattered by the compliments, but at the same time, I thought it was kind of funny. It felt weird, but at least I knew now that I had a chance in the industry. Everyone at the party was partying and drinking. Most people were too wasted to make sense of anything and were clearly having the time of their lives.

Richard Hardman's parents were away, so that's why they were having this sleepover party, basically. Carol's parents thought she was at my house, and my parents thought I was at Carol's house. It was the perfect alibi, and we managed to get away with it. After all, what else could you expect from teenage girls in their prime? This was bound to happen sooner or later, and to be frank; I enjoyed the party.

By the end of the evening, Richard Hardman asked me, "Would you like to see the house?" He was eyeing me throughout the night. Everywhere I looked, I saw him there, gazing at me with deep admiration. I could see that he wanted me right there and then. He would always show up wherever I was standing, which was quite flattering. When he realized that the party was about to end, he finally mustered up the courage and approached me.

I responded by saying, "Yes," and without a moment's hesitation, Richard Hardman started showing me around the house. Throughout the tour, he charmed me with his words and opulence. Got to give credit to Richard; he had a way with words, and he was quite convincing. The tour finished when we reached his parents' bedroom suite, which was very luxurious, to say the least. It had these long, fancy curtains and numerous paintings by renaissance artists. One could easily see that the room itself was worth millions of dollars. And, in all honesty, I was sold from the get-go.

In a matter of seconds, Richard grabbed me from behind and started kissing me passionately. He then carried me in his arms and gently put me in his parent's bed. It was so exhilarating that I completely lost sight of Carol, Billy, and even the party. I was fully engrossed in that passionate moment. The mood was set, and we started to make love to each other (have sex).

Before this, being the friend I was, I personally made sure that Carol and Billy spent the night together. However, Carol was a bit of what I considered "a cock tease." What do I mean by this? I mean that Carol wanted to have sex but didn't want to be perceived as a slut. She wanted her man to be absolutely obsessed with her before she got in bed with him. It didn't make much sense to me, but every girl is different, and Carol was one of these cock teasing girls.

At that point, the entirety of my sex education consisted of *Playboy* and *Penthouse* magazines that we would find when we were babysitting. This material was usually tucked under a bed or a mattress or something or in the husband's closet.

We would go through that material and try to find information that could prove useful later on. I didn't have any interest in the pictures but was very interested in the articles and the columnists. Back in those days, there was *The Happy Hooker*, who wrote a column about sexual relationships and the stigma attached to them. It wanted to liberate the commonly held conservative notion about sex and make it more appealing to the masses.

Other than *The Happy Hooker*, *Cosmopolitan Magazine* also wrote prolifically regarding sex and the single girl. At this time, things were changing so quickly and dramatically that many people couldn't even believe what was going on. Most people were trying to wrap their heads around these changes, and by the time they made sense of it, the event or situation had already changed. It was a very radical time, and it allowed us to have the sexual freedom we enjoy today. During this period, I read the *Kama Sutra*. I also read a fabulous book, *The Joy of Sex*, which was very much about free love and group sex and is probably still in publication today.

However, practically speaking, I had no experience with sex. This was mainly because I didn't have many dates in high school. Though, I do remember one particular instance where a guy took me to the movies. We were watching the movie, and his hand was kind of in my lap.

Before long, he started moving his fingers around, and in all honesty, it turned me on a lot. I had no idea what to do. All I knew for sure was that I was embarrassed and thought I shouldn't be doing this. Though, I didn't know how to stop it. After that incident, I never went out with him again. If I am being completely honest, I had a few dates where we would, as my mother called it, "neck," lots of making out and kissing.

Moreover, I spent five days a week in New York modeling, going to see photographers, and doing numerous interviews. This hobby of mine introduced me to a whole new world of men wanting me, following me around, and even hiring private detectives to figure out where I lived to see if they could go out with me. It was a strange but heady time for me, but frankly, I enjoyed the extra attention.

Prior to this encounter with Richard Hardman, I had only kissed a boy a couple of times and really didn't have any clue what to do in the act. Slowly, Richard Hardman started to work on me, and I let him take my virginity.

Now that I recall, during this time, Carol and I were actually in a kind of race as to who would lose their virginity first. I have a very competitive nature, and so naturally, I wanted to be first. Plus, I was a year older than Carol. This implied that I HAD to have sex before Carol, no matter the costs.

On the other end of the spectrum, Richard Hardman had not been with a virgin before. I'm quite sure of this because he didn't really know what he was doing. He just kept on trying to get his cock inside me until it was practically the middle of the night. It hurt. It was CLEARLY not working. Then, thank God, he got the idea to get some Vaseline. This turned out to be a complete game changer, and suddenly he was in me, and we were fucking nonstop. I don't remember much after that; I probably passed out.

The next morning, the sheets were a complete mess, filled with blood and bodily fluids. I'm not sure this really happened or whether I've remembered this from the scene in *The Godfather*, where after the consummation of the marriage, they hang the sheet out the window to display the obvious signs of someone losing their virginity. It was as bloody and disgusting as you'd expect and not what I thought it would be at all.

What I do know is that by the time we got to the barn, word had spread like wildfire. I was teased like hell by all the guys at the barn. I was quite embarrassed but also a little proud because I had been the geekiest kid in my high school. It was a very large high school. And suddenly, people were telling me how much of a catch I was. It tremendously boosted my self-confidence and allowed me to see who I truly was.

Through the photographs, I could see that I was actually beautiful in the right situation, with the right makeup and my contact lenses, etc. Hence, I adopted these changes and moved on in my life. With time, my self-confidence grew exponentially, and I accepted my being, my beauty, and my desires. From that point on, I had multiple sexual relationships that I enjoyed without any moral qualms or regrets whatsoever, and I urge everyone reading this book to follow this ideal.

Chapter 2:

James Rector

Meeting Michelle Mustain and Shane Ericson changed my life forever. I was exposed to a whole new world. This all happened when I got to watch Shane school the young horses that he got from the Belmont sales, or the ones he and James Rector shipped from Europe. Shane had performed in all three major Olympic equestrian competitions and was very skilled in his craft. I think Shane and James Rector were the first ones to ship horses from Europe. James Rector told Shane about all of these horses that English farmers would raise, fox hunt a little bit, and eventually fatten up and sell. He, Shane, and Michelle went to Europe and to England and came back with the first planeload of horses, which Shane started to train.

He could be tough on the horses, but he was brilliant. They would make up these horses. Shane was getting quite a name for himself as a horse trainer and horse dealer. Michelle was his ground assistant. Together, they would work on this. Besides being Shane's partner, James' job was that he really showed Richard and Michelle the ropes of the very sophisticated world of New York.

Also, because James Rector previously had a very successful business in the city, he taught them how to schmooze customers, show them the horses, then invite them out for dinner, and hopefully close the deal or at least make a great impression. He taught them to dress. Their uniform was custom-made monogrammed shirts` with blue jeans and Gucci loafers. Michelle could really carry it off, as could Shane. In the barn, they would wear boots to ride horses.

During one of these evenings, Michelle suggested that I should go out with James Rector. When I heard her suggestion, I immediately thought, I'm 17, and I'm like, he's 48, which he was probably lying about his age, and he was older than that. At the time, I shrugged off the idea completely, not knowing what was in store for me in the not-so-distant future. Boy, was I wrong!

One night, we came back from dinner. I went down to my friend Shelly and Sharon's apartment, the groom's apartment, and got ready for bed. I was sleeping on the pull-out couch in the lounge. I went up there, and James Rector was waiting for me and started to kiss me. He said, "Well, you must want to be with me. You brushed your teeth."

Hearing this, I started laughing and said, "1 brush my teeth every night."

From that point on, we started exploring each other. James Rector was extremely experienced. He'd been married twice. His last wife was someone he found in Oklahoma. James' business was commercial productions. He was very wealthy at the time. He drove a dark green Rolls-Royce Corniche Convertible with saddle interior. James Rector and I started commuting back and forth between his townhouse in New York and the cottage in New Hope, Pennsylvania, a couple of miles away from where Shane and Michelle's farm was.

If I'm being honest, I never had bad sex with James Rector, ever. I don't think James even knew what bad sex was. On the contrary, he knew just what a girl wanted and gave it to her in splendid fashion. The way he used his hands, the way he'd roll you over, and the way he'd take you was a turn-on in itself. However, he only wanted to take you after telling you. He knew I liked to be told what to do.

And, sure enough, I would follow his commands through and through. He had no inhibitions. I remember we would fuck anywhere, in whatever condition we were in, and carry through with the act ecstatically.

At times, I don't think we behaved appropriately when we were in the act. There were times when we would fuck indiscriminately, irrespective of the fact James' daughters were upstairs in the cottage in New Hope. They were probably traumatized for life, but we didn't care. We were having the time of our lives, and we didn't care who was watching, listening, or seeing us in the heat of passion.

When his daughters would come home for the weekend, they would stay in the cottage on the second floor, and we'd be on the first floor fucking our brains out. I'm sure they could hear us, but James had no awareness of this, nor did I. Frankly, I didn't think they could hear us, and I was too busy being with James to care.

Often, we'd go over to his neighbor's pool. Normally, water and I don't do well when it comes to fucking, but James knew just what to do. He'd put me up on the side of the pool, licked my pussy, and made sure I was hot and wet. After that, we coupled together and fucked in the pool.

There was a time we went to New York. We visited Jim Henson's, the guy who founded the Muppets house. Jim was an old-time friend of James. Us going there was James recovering from Pamela's sudden exit from his life. So, he wanted to show me off the new flavor in town, and we had no compunction or sense of where we should or shouldn't fuck.

One day, there was a group of people in the living room. Yet still, James and I sneaked off to the den and fucked hard on Jim Henson's sofa, which then left, as Michelle would call it, "the wet". James just turned the cushion over, and we simply went back and joined this other group as if nothing had happened.

In retrospect, I now know this was totally marking his territory and repairing his damaged ego, but I loved every second of it. I was the star of the show. He treated me like a goddess. We went to fabulous malls, festivals, galas, and other lavish places together. The time we spent was always incredible.

Also, looking back, he took me under his wing, and I became his next project. He dressed me up and bought me designer clothes. Then, he would show me off. I spent the summer with James. We would play James' favorite music. I think there were eight tracks in those days. We would go back and forth and spend time with Shane and Michelle. Then, James Rector's ex-wife ran off to Europe and left him heartbroken. I was the replacement. He started buying me clothes and even gave me Pamela's clothes, his former wife. We were perfectly matched for sex. James Rector adored me physically, and eventually, the connection became emotional. He made love to me on his king-sized bed in Turtle Bay.

We had a heavenly summer going to amazing restaurants in New York, where we were given private spots in the side yard. Everyone knew who James was. He was the one who educated me about French food and wine. In all honesty, French wine was very heady. But sadly, I was off to college, and James Rector pushed me out of the nest. Things proceeded from there for me as I moved back to Montclair and went to The New School. I was on the periphery of various drug businesses. Normally, I would go with James in his Rolls-Royce from New Hope to New York, back and forth.

At the end of the summer, I made a really foolish move and brought James to my parents' house, claiming that he was just this rich guy from the barn. We were going to New York and then back out to the farm. Anyone could see sparks flying off between the two of us, but I didn't notice. When we're 17, we have a tendency to think that our parents don't know anything.

Instantly, my father picked up on the cues and instructed James to come out back. I knew my father; he was a black Irish, no doubt about it. My dad was the all Catholic quarterback for Massachusetts when he was 15 and later joined the navy with fake papers. He got to see major action against the Japanese and was battle-hardened. In other words, he was very fearsome. I later found out from James that he took him in the back and pushed him up against the wall. He then proceeded to grab him by the balls and said,

"You are going to make sure my daughter goes to college this fall. She will not continue modeling and living with you."

Eventually, James and I left. James was a little shaken up from that fiasco. My father could be really intimidating, let me tell you, and James made sure I went to school one way or another. Another thing I like to point out is that James had a knack for buying and selling Rolls-Royces. He'd buy them in New York and then take them to California, where the people didn't worry about salt damage. Then, he would sell them at a reasonable profit and buy another Rolls-Royce. This was one of his little side businesses. Sometime later, I found out that he had taken a model with him on a trip to California to sell his car and didn't tell me.

When he came back, he was all apologetic and making excuses that she meant nothing to him, and he said something like, "She was not interesting and being with her was like reading the newspaper throughout the trip."

I was very hurt. Then, he took me aside and said, "You're too smart not to go to college and attend veterinary school. I can't afford to put you through college and vet school. I think we should break up, and you should go off to college."

Hearing these words broke my heart. I was deeply hurt, and I, fortunately, learned a valuable lesson. From then on, I was always very particular about who I was with. If I found out anyone was lying to me, as they frequently would, not mentioning the wives they had or girlfriends just to be with me, I would simply avoid them. Despite this, I had some special men that I would bend over backward, such as James or Mike.

It's hard to really put my finger on what caused the magic between James and myself. It was a heady time. I gave my heart to him completely and thought we would be together forever. I had no earthly idea what was about to transpire. He just had this way of dominating with his physicality and his love of sex. He made you feel so wanted. He accepted you physically on every level; you didn't have to worry about him NOT pushing the right buttons. He knew what women expected of him, and boy, did he deliver.

Other than that, the man loved to go down on you. He loved to use his hands everywhere, especially your breasts. He would handle your breasts by gently massaging them and then tweaking them. He would do this back and forth until you got wet. In short, James covered all the bases.

In my view, the thing that made James stand out was that he was super masculine but very sensitive at the same time. He had this incredible wit and personality, and his innate talent for telling tales made you laugh hysterically. In all honesty, I feel so lucky to have had James in my life and the fact that our relationship lasted as long as it did. I'd like to point out that we had been lovers on and off for the time span of 25 to 30 years. Many would come and go, but he was always mine.

I absolutely adored the man, and he adored me, He was a rascal, a really naughty boy, but it wasn't my problem. He was mine first. Even though he'd fucked me over, didn't take me to Europe as he promised, and broke up with me to foolishly try and land a horse dealing business without Richard.

At this pivotal moment, I recall telling him that his idea wouldn't work and that he needed someone like Shane, first of all, to ride horses, train them and bring them along. I also pointed out the fact that he needed to interact with the other horse dealers. That's what people were buying, the Shane label.

An interesting thing about James was that he fought in World War II and was shot in the elbow. He could only bend his left arm at a right angle. One of his great charms was that he was a fabulous raconteur and could tell stories for hours of things he had done in his life, all the way back when he was just a poor child in Detroit.

Before long, he found himself fighting in World War II, getting shot, being hospitalized, fucking the nurses, or so he said. It probably was true knowing him. Then, he used the GI Bill to go to art school in France. By the time he came home, he had founded his commercial production firm, which was very successful. He had a townhouse in Turtle Bay, which was immensely beautiful that he had decorated himself. Almost all the walls were made of some sort of fabric.

In fact, a number of his commercials were in MoMA, the Museum of Modern Arts, permanent film collection. He had a minor heart problem, and this freaked him out. He sold his business and spent all his time at the horse farm, his cottage, or in Turtle Bay. Then, he met me, and you know how things worked out from then.

Talking about betrayals, let me point out another person who gravely disappointed me, Julia. Initially, I thought Julia, who was a snake in the grass,but she would become one of my best friends at the horse shows. I had defended her when Mark Dennis, her boyfriend, wanted to shoot her when he had just won the National Horse Show Open Jumper Championship for the year. I don't know what it was exactly called back then. Today we'd call it Horse of the Year or Grand Prix Horse of the year.

Julia was either fucking around or bullshitting with one of Shane's best friends. Shane rented Charlie O's under Madison Square Garden for an open bar party. From where he got the money, I have no earthly idea. He was probably doing something shady or offhanded. I remember him totally freaking out. He came up to me and asked, "Issy, where is she?"

I remember replying, "1 don't know," even though I did know where she was. I wasn't going to tell him, knowing his reputation.

After hearing my reply, he retorted bluntly, "You know I've killed people."

I replied confidently, "I suspected that might be true."

He said, "I'll kill them if they're together."

I responded anxiously, "I don't think you have to worry about that." To tell the truth, I was shaking the entire time. His presence was enough to frighten even the bravest men. He was scary and had a famously bad temper. No one knew when he would explode and cause irreprehensible damage. So, you can see how much I cared for Julia. But, alas, some people are simply not decent. They cannot be grateful for anything or anyone.

I literally saved Julia, but she didn't return the favor. She stole James from me, saying that she could do the horse business with him. They'd be great, and everything would be wonderful, and rainbows would be shining out their ass. It turned out to be a total failure. He lost a lot of money, and Julia's behavior got weirder and weirder.

James once told me a story about how he had friends over at his new house in New Hope. He finally had a new house. It was really nice. She would go upstairs and use a really loud vibrator. She would use this while these guests were downstairs and completely embarrass James. I don't know what point she was trying to prove. From that time on, I was really strict about wanting to know if I knew someone had a girlfriend or wife, I wouldn't be with them. I got hurt so badly when she talked James into going with her for this bullshit idea.

Sorry, I am going off on a tangent here, so back to James. James and I continued to be lovers for years. James loved to have phone sex with me. He found my voice very sexy, as do others. He'd call me up, and I could tell. He'd start breathing heavily, and I could tell he was whacking himself off, which sometimes was titillating while other times annoying. But I always loved to talk to him and find out what he was up to.

Usually, we'd talk about his daughter, who was active in the New York fashion scene. She went on to marry Calvin Klein, who was bisexual. Calvin Klein was pretty famous in the fashion scene, but he couldn't come out. This was the '70s, and everyone was worried about AIDs. So, you can imagine how scared James was for her. We often talked about her and that whole crazy fashion business.

I was doing this while working all the time and showing my horse or horses. I didn't have time to fool around. In any case, I cannot express how wonderful the '60s and '70s were. I don't even know how to describe this era. Because of this era, I got to experience what I did and developed such tremendous relationships. And rest assured, James did not want to be without me at a certain point. We would get together, and the time we spent would be phenomenal. If you'd ask me, we were meant to be together. Although fate clearly had other plans. In the end, our decisions are what shape us and determine our future, so be careful when making certain key decisions in your life. All I can do now is reminisce and cherish the moments that James and I shared together, along with my several other exploits.

Don't worry; we have a lot to cover.

Chapter 3:

Last of the Canadian Lovers

The first among the list that I will speak about just recently came to mind when I traveled up here to Canada. My cousin got married in the late 70s in Canada, which was wonderful. Before long, I was introduced by my cousin to this great friend of hers. He was in charge of looking after me. This meant that I had to spend the next ten days with him. My cousin's friend was true to his word; he supervised me very carefully.

He had this incredible wood-fired sauna house that had an anteroom with a great big truck tire with fabrics stretched over it like a trampoline. We used this room as a place to cool off since it was situated between the sauna and the freezing-cold lake. Perhaps the tire's greatest contribution was that it was a great place to fuck.

In all honesty, he was a master fucker. He was large but not too large. He cooked me dinner and had an incredible collection of antique wooden boats. We would often use one of them at night to look at the stars and fondle each other. Then, we would go back to the sauna. The only negative thing was that by the end of the ten days, I had become really tired. I was sore to such an extent that on the last night we spent together, I didn't fuck him. I know you won't believe me, but I really was too sore to fuck. We had a very awkward conversation afterward and became really distant.

I didn't see him for a few decades until recently when I moved back here to Canada. Nowadays, I see him at the club occasionally. But he's not overly friendly with me. Perhaps, he misinterpreted me not fucking him on the last day we spent together. Maybe he thought I did it on purpose to dump him.

However, this couldn't be further from the truth. I actually was too sore; he had drained the life out of me. The previous nine days had taken a toll on me, and I made a conscious decision not to have sex with him. Now that I recall, I think the deep conversations we had on the boat might have gotten to him. Who knows. In any case, he was great and one of the three greatest Canadian lovers I ever had.

Chronologically, I realize that I didn't discuss when I got sent to Canada to be "civilized" by my aunt and uncle. They were the two people I adored, but I was a little afraid of them as well. My aunt was very formidable. She was the head steward, or rule keeper, for international shows.

There's something called the Pony Club for young kids to ride in and learn all about riding and horsemanship. You have to take care of your horse or pony, and you have to clean your saddles and bridles and all that. In other words, you're in charge of all of the horse care. It starts at, I think, Level D, and the highest level you can get is an A.

My aunt was in charge of the Pony Club. Besides founding the Pony Club in Canada, she also judged all of the kids whether they would pass their A-level Pony Club Certificate or not. Believe me, when I say it, this was quite an honor and difficult to do. She also had the privilege of teaching most of the Canadian future Olympics Team. She would keep an eye out for guys getting the girls to do their work for them. And she would catch them at every instant. Nothing got past my aunt.

Later on, in my college years, she would lock horns with the head coach for the American team, who was always trying to cheat. The Americans were always trying to cheat in those days because the rules were very loose in America about what you could do with and to horses. They would deliberately not complete their jumps or come up with some excuse. They did this to steal the competition from right under the Canadians' noses. It was really frustrating, but we had to deal with it one way or another. In any case, my aunt was really cool.

Through her, I first met him when I was in 7th grade. He was just coming back from winning the gold medal in show jumping at the Mexican '68 Olympics. This man was none other than Mike, one of the greatest lovers of my entire life. He was also teased by a couple of his friends because of his gold medal. They used to refer to him as "Daisy May." However, this didn't shatter his confidence. He was still the stunning, handsome gold medalist right there for the taking.

But at this point, I was like the geekiest 7th or 8th grader. My aunt came down to see the big horseshow at the old Madison Square Garden before they tore it down. In fact, it was the last year of its operation, and the show moved to the new Madison Square Garden. I still remember that moment so vividly, as if it happened only yesterday.

Mike Hunt walks past us, sees my aunt, and immediately comes over and sits down next to her. At the time, all I could think about was: *I'm just a horse-crazy kid. Here's this incredible international rider in the red coat. Do I actually have a chance? Will he listen to me? Will he be interested in me?*

Mike Hunt always wore rose-colored glasses. Nobody quite understood why he wore those glasses. It was a mystery that was still not solved. In my opinion, I think he wore those shades because he was shy. Whenever somebody asked him about the glasses, he always told them he had sensitive eyes. In any case, glasses or not, I had a mad crush on Mike. In fact, he was one of my first crushes, probably my first crush.

In the fall, I was sent to Canada; I attended the Royal Winter Fair in Toronto. I had gone to show my horse, and my parents hoped I would be civilized by my aunt and uncle in Canada. However, I think I was beyond being civilized. I was showing my horse in the professional division against all the Olympic riders. The fences were four-foot-six high, which was extremely high. It was really high in general. I think five-foot-three was the maximum height for Olympics show jumping. I had shown my horse locally in the regular working hunter division in New Jersey and jumped four-foot fences.

My horse could jump the moon, and he was honest as anything, an incredible horse. Let me remind you that I had no trainer. What's more, I did all my own braids. During this time, my aunt hooked me up with a great family of girls called the Carpenters. I had their support, and I could count on them for anything my horse or I needed. I prepared for the competition at their farm, and it was really fun.

Before long, I went off to the show. My aunt was busy the whole time between social events and stewarding. I would walk in the ring without ever having seen the course and pick up a canter. My horse would canter around and jump everything like a star. I would make some beginner mistakes for that level. Even though we put in a lot of effort, we only got some low ribbons. Yet still, it was a tremendous accomplishment.

Now that I look back, I actually got to know Mike as an adult woman. In those days, these big international horse shows had great parties, and you had to dress up for the occasion. You had to look like a million bucks. Otherwise, the chances were you wouldn't get in. That was why I spent a few extra minutes perfecting my look.

People were all dressed up in ballgowns and gorgeous clothes, with men in tuxedos and formal foxhunting dancing cutaways. There was no way we would miss these parties. I'd go, and my friends would go. We'd all sneak into these parties. Free liquor, free food, what more could a college kid want? By the time I got to the party, Mike had started flirting with me. He knew who I was and would refer to me as "sexy Sandy's niece."

We started flirting, and sparks were flying. He was a well-known cocksman of many lovers. He was probably the first truly great lover I ever had, except for James. I mean, he was in a completely different stratosphere in terms of lovemaking. He'd come by and, just in passing, subtly say, "You want to meet me in my room in ten minutes?"

To which I said, "Yes." I wasn't quite sure what would happen, but I had my hopes. Sure enough, we went to his room and had passionate sex. He was so athletic and strong that, for the life of me, I couldn't find any flaw in him whatsoever. It was as if he was a perfect specimen. He was undoubtedly every girl's dream, and I had him all to myself.

To this day, I can clearly remember our passionate encounter. It was simply amazing. He knew what I expected from him and delivered through and through. As soon as I reached his room, he started to fuck me, kiss me, go down on me, and do everything I could possibly want. Then, I was on top. He turned me over but did not, like most guys, disengage. As I mentioned previously, he was strong enough to hold us together. He then pulled me over to the side of the bed, picked me up, twirled me around six times, and then lay me back down.

Truth be told, I cannot describe how fantastic this encounter was. But, for the sake of the readers, I will try to simplify it as much as I can. In simple terms, Mike fucked the hell out of me while never disengaging. It was quite something. He definitely knew what he was doing.

We spent the rest of that Indoors—I should describe "Indoors." Indoors were the international horse shows that—four actually in those days—people came from Europe to compete in. There were national teams and flags everywhere, and they had very high-level Olympic quality pretty much all around. America and Canada competed fiercely for who would win. However, I had other responsibilities as well. Responsibilities that I couldn't possibly ignore, especially my education.

At that point, I had gotten all my books because I was supposed to be in college. However, instead of studying and living up to my parents' expectations, I was at the horseshow, staying with my new best friend, Amy Connor. Mike and I were at every party, every night, following the same schtick. It had almost become a routine of sorts. Every time, he would come up to me and say, "You want to meet me in my room?"

As expected, I would comply and go to his room and have passionate love.

After the first night, I was even more eager to pursue this. But I was terrified that my aunt was going to find out. One day, I had all my books, and I was going to study, and I walked past the Canadian team. They were all sitting like birds of a feather on a fence rail. I walked past them, and Mike abruptly said, "Hi, Tiger. This is sexy Sandy's niece."

They all started laughing and snickering almost immediately. It was as if they were expecting Mike to react this way. He'd obviously told them what our relationship was, and they couldn't possibly ignore a moment like this. Embarrassed, I turned bright red and kept on walking. I didn't quite know what to say at that point.

The next fall, Mike was again back on the team. It was Indoors. We'd just picked up where we had left off. I hadn't talked to him or seen him since the previous Indoors. He was wonderful. He could do things to you that no one else ever did. He was so sexy. I will always remember my times with him over those two years. However, as soon as the two years ended, I didn't see him again until I was in my 60s.

Sadly, he had developed dementia and had no memory of me and our two years together. I was at a horseshow in Canada, recognized him, and talked to him, but it was like there was no one home, really. It was very sad. Unfortunately, this also happened with another great lover of mine, James Rector, who has since died. The last time I talked to him, he was suffering from Alzheimer's or Dementia or whatever. He didn't remember me. Our affair had been much more serious than the one with Mike, yet he couldn't remember a thing. It was kind of heartbreaking, but it wasn't his fault, really.

In a nutshell, these were my Canadian adventures. I guess I covered both Muskoka and the Royal Winter Fair. Oh wait, there was this other guy as well. This other guy picked me up at the horseshow. I had lost my keys, and he was kind enough to drive me home. I had locked my keys in the car.

Quite frankly, I became an expert at using my hanger to open the car door. Why? Because every other day, I locked my keys in the car. It was annoying, and it happened so many times that I lost track. Anyway, getting back, this guy offered to drive me home. My home was my aunt and uncle's farm, about an hour away from the show. I was living with my aunt and uncle in their home. This guy and I were at the bottom of an 80-acre horse farm and driving to a long winding driveway up the restored farmhouse. Eventually, we parked at the bottom of the driveway, and somehow in his car, we started fucking. It happened so suddenly that, for a moment, I didn't believe this was actually happening. I thought it was one of those wild dreams, but surely it wasn't.

He was so moved by me that he followed me back to New Jersey and got a job with Mark's barn, which was right next door to my barn. At the same time, he'd drive 45 minutes to an hour down to my house in Montclair to see me at night. I guess something I was doing was charming him. I remember he had the strangest technique, which no one had ever used on me before or since. He'd blow up your vagina and uterus with air.

As I gained more knowledge and experience over the years, I finally realized what he was doing. He was trying to make me cum by stimulating the way the uterus and vagina balloon out. This is what happens right before the girl is about to orgasm. In short, he knew what he was doing, and I have to give him credit for that. Our affair lasted for a while.

We'd go to the movies and do a lot of stuff together. During this time, the kids had converted the dining room, which was adjacent to the front hall and library. It shared one chimney for three fireplaces into a kind of rec room. That's where we would retire to. We thought nothing, or I thought nothing of fucking him.

As the crow flies, I was probably 30 feet from my parents. Yet, they didn't take any notice whatsoever. Again, as I had mentioned already, my parents drank a lot, smoked a lot of cigarettes, and probably realized by now that they had pretty much lost control of my behavior. But I don't know whether they ever admitted that to themselves.

At any rate, he finally went back to Canada. That was fine. I didn't love him. I didn't even really lust after him that strongly. It was an interesting experience for sure but not that impactful. I think he thought I had a lot of money. The rumor in Canada was that he only went out with rich girls. Not all of my affairs were serious. I had quite a few very nonserious affairs, as you'll come to know in future chapters. Trust me; you haven't seen anything yet.

Chapter 4:

Terry Cooper

Oh, how do I even begin to describe Terry Cooper? He was really something else. I can vividly remember each and every moment we spent together. Yes, the memories are as bright as day. In fact, I would say that Terry is definitely one of the top ten, if not the top five, lovers in my life. Now that I look back, I met him when I was living in New Jersey. At the time, my dad was very sick. It was a difficult emotional time for me, and I was bored to tears other than my college work.

I was sitting up in our great room when I noticed something. These two guys started walking toward the back door, which was the standard thing. These two young men would walk in, say hi to my parents and a few cordial things, and then go down to the basement to the drug den. Upon closer inspection, I realized that one of these boys looked familiar. After contemplating for a few seconds, I figured out who he was. One of the guys was the younger brother of a good friend of mine. From what I understand, he was a real weirdo and later died of a heart attack from too much cocaine.

His friend, on the other hand, was absolutely gorgeous. He had dark red hair and a bandana tied up like a pirate on his head. He really stood out, and I became attracted to him right there and then. I'd forgotten what else he was wearing. But what I do remember was being instantaneously taken with him, and he with me. There was an instant connection that we both couldn't possibly ignore. And as a result, he didn't take long to approach me. Before long, Terry asked me out later that week. I got dressed like I was going on a date in New York.

When Terry arrived, he was dressed casually from top to bottom. In a way, I was sort of relieved. I thought, *At least, he is genuine.* In any case, our date went on, and I got to know Terry a little better. I looked gorgeous. Because, at this point, I was modeling and going to college. I was doing stuff but living at home in Montclair, where I had some friends who were not at college or whatever. It was a pretty mundane and boring period for me, and I was glad Terry was there to spice it up a little.

In all honesty, our relationship was a surefire example of instantaneous love. Later that week, Terry took me out for a second time. The moment Terry and I locked eyes, I could feel my heart pounding and sparks flying. It was truly amazing. I remember him taking me out to a friend's apartment. She was older and totally not attractive. As a result, I wasn't at all threatened by her. From what I understood, Terry and this girl were nothing more than friends. I knew his kind, girls like me, and this girl was definitely not like me.

She, apparently, would let Terry come and hang out at her apartment and perhaps also use one of the bedrooms. At any rate, Terry and I hung out there with lots of sparing back and forth. He could be full of himself with good reason. He didn't like taking no for an answer. He wasn't going to back down for anyone. And sure enough, I was about to learn this fact.

He ended up taking me home despite the fact I did not want to wait. At the time, I was in full lioness mode. I can be quite a predator. And my sights were set on Terry. I wasn't going to rest until I had him. We ended up going out again. I think we just drove around in my mother's car. Terry went to the boys' private school in town. I think he was just starting to get ready for college in Boston.

Terry was smart, but he wasn't brilliant. As we got to know each other, I later found out that he was actually an adopted child. In fact, after that, we spent even more time together. We became lovers, as I'm sure that's a huge surprise to everybody reading this book.

He was fabulous. I mean, he was younger than I was, but Lord knows how many girls he had bedded in high school. He was a total charmer and knew what every girl wanted. At the same time, Terry could be rough. He could be demanding but in a good way. It was all so sexy. He was definitely in command. He was the alpha dog and acted like it every time we engaged in passionate lovemaking.

Eventually, we ended up going back to his dad's house. Before long, in the dining room, on the oriental rug under the dining room table, to be more specific, we started fucking like crazy. Right then, in the heat of passion, his dad walked into the room. Luckily, it was dark. He immediately said, "Is someone there? Is that you, Terry? I swear I heard a sound down here. Was that you? C'mon, boy, speak up."

He waited for a few seconds, and when he didn't hear anything back, he went back to bed. It was fairly late in the night, and I figured he was too exhausted to conduct a thorough search. He yawned quite a bit and returned back to his room. Thanks to Terry's dad, Terry and I finally had a chance to take a breather. Truth be told, it was very hard not to pant in light of the wonderful fucking we had undergone. And sure enough, we had almost reached that point. It was intense, and I'm not exaggerating one bit.

Let me also point out that I loved to suck Terry's cock. Sex with Terry was just so raw and passionate that nothing seemed off-limits. Make no mistake; I loved it. Terry also did his part in pleasuring me. He would go down on me every time we had sex. We had engaged in all sorts of positions. We did it on the floor, on the couch, and of course, on the bed. No stone was left unturned.

However, despite all that, he wasn't my greatest lover. Yet still, he was pretty close in my book. Terry was definitely up there with James, not emotionally but physically. Also, he was 17 years old or something like that. This meant that he could fuck forever. He was a teenager; his hormones were running wild. And, in this age, every person, whether the individual is a boy or girl, has copious amounts of energy. I mean, fucking was fun with Terry. We would laugh, joke, and tease each other on a regular basis. He didn't take life so seriously, and I think that was the thing that I found most attractive about him. He was a kid; after all, life was simply a casual, fun endeavor for him. And I absolutely loved his carefree, fun-loving, and passionate attitude.

One night, we were in the jacuzzi and indoor pool at my house and Terry took the cushions and made a bed from them. This was a very weird idea, but when you're fucking somebody else's brains out, you can expect a great deal of weirdness. It worked, and he got me up and gently placed me on the cushions. Before long, we started fucking. They seemed sturdy, but we fucked so hard on the cushions that they shifted. As a result, we both got rug burns from the indoor/outdoor carpeting that surrounded the pool. That was hard to explain but rest assured, it did happen. We felt the burn for a couple of weeks, although, looking back, it was worth it.

He then graduated from college. We had stayed as lovers for a number of years. I went to college in California after my father died. At any rate, Terry and I eventually didn't see each other for a while. Though, in retrospect, we were not apart for that long. Terry had gotten a job which meant that he would be busy throughout the day. He had also moved to New Rochelle in Westchester, NY. So, naturally, our interactions were now fairly limited.

One day out of the blue, he called me up and told me that he wanted me now. As you'd imagine, I complied with his wish. I got in my car and drove up there. By the time I reached his home, I distinctly remember Terry rushing toward me, picking me up, and immediately taking me to the bedroom. It was as if he hadn't fucked in a while and couldn't wait to get inside me.

He was quite rough with me. It was almost like a pseudo-rape, but it was very sexy. He was working something out during this time. Things were not going well for him at work. I believe it had something to do with his female boss. I think she was giving him a hard time, and quite frankly, he could do nothing about it. As I mentioned before, he didn't like losing control. And when he did, he had to take it back.

However, let me clarify that anything Terry did was well within the bounds of what I was comfortable with. I just loved to fuck, suck, and be with him. It was just so much fun. He was very strong and just a masterful lover. He loved to kiss, and every time we made love, he kissed me all over. It was very scintillating, and I deeply enjoyed every moment of it. Once again, I'd like to say that he was definitely, probably, in the top five list of my favorite lovers. This, in itself, is quite an accomplishment.

Coming back, sometime after that encounter, he called me up again. He had a new job. He had now moved to northwestern Connecticut and invited me up for the weekend. I was thrilled. I had been languishing in Montclair for so long that, frankly, it was quite depressing. So, without a moment's hesitation, I packed my bag, borrowed my mother's car, and immediately headed up there. We had fun and repeated our usual antics.

Sometime later, he had a friend come over. They were watching football and stuff, but I wasn't at all interested in that. On the contrary, I was interested in Terry. Eventually, he invited me into his bedroom. Actually, I think it might have been me who lured him inside. In any case, we spent the night together with Terry and myself, pleasuring each other and having a great time.

The next morning, Terry got up, and his friend got up as well. They both came into the room. Then, all of a sudden, Terry asked me a rather peculiar question. Terry wanted to know whether I wanted to have a threesome. Frankly, I was not at all attracted to his friend, and so I said, "No, I really don't want to."

His friend didn't make this an issue. Far from it, he took it in a very light and casual way. To be fair, I didn't outrightly say that I rejected the threesome idea because I didn't find Terry's friend attractive. I simply said, "No," and everybody accepted my decision, no drama, no nothing. Both he and his friend were real gentlemen, and I was glad to be with Terry every step of the way.

Afterward, Terry and I spent the early afternoon making love some more and pleasuring each other as we had learned to do. By this time, we had learned what the other wanted so well. It was breathtaking, and if given a chance, I would relive those moments in a second. Then, I drove home.

There was just something magical about him. He had magical hands. Terry was the magic man as depicted in the illustrious song *Magic Man*, no doubt about it. Even now, in my later years and after numerous exploits, I treasure the time we spent together and wouldn't trade it for anything.

Chapter 5:

Kyle Singer

I need to distinguish between each lover and the impact they had on my life. So, bear with me and enjoy the journey ahead. Here, I will talk about my Canadian lover—Kyle Singer. Let's begin.

Kyle, also one of the greatest lovers I've ever had, was quite a character, but that's not the reason he became a part of my book. Rest assured, there are many hijinks involved in this chapter.

I met Kyle at my favorite island, Blueberry Island. I was out on one of the rock outcroppings, just looking at the beautiful lake. It was so extraordinary that, for a while, I had completely forgotten where I was and what I was doing.

Then, all of a sudden, this group arrived at the island. It was a very noisy group, older than me a bit. I was still quite young. I was 17. In fact, I had just turned 17. So, I was basically a teenage girl who had much to learn. Kyle, on the other hand, was very experienced in dealing with women. You could tell by his confidence and the way he walked, talked, and looked at a girl. In other words, he knew what turned a woman on. It didn't take long for him to come over to where I was and begin chatting me up. Whatever he did, it worked. Because, in just a few moments, I became attracted to him and our casual chat became really intense.

In our conversation, we found out that my grandfather's cottage was pretty close to his family's cottage. Let me point out that I almost never have been picked up in my life. Pick-up has never been my style, nor do I usually fall for these tricks. But that's what happened with Kyle. What can I say? He was pretty skilled at it. However, I did not let my guard down immediately. First, I got to know him and his friends a little better. I had to make sure he wasn't a creep. So, I put him to the test, and he succeeded.

Sometime later, everybody decided that they were going to another friend who was building a log cabin cottage on a little island. This friend had a floatplane, who, strangely enough, I bedded decades later.

Eventually, we all ended up in another friend's boathouse. Kyle was a pro-hockey player in Toronto and had a thick mustache and curly hair, which was brown-blonde. He was very good-looking. We resumed our little talk in the boathouse, and it got really interesting really quickly.

As I remember, I was fully clad in a bikini. In a few seconds, Kyle started to put the make on me. I was not opposed to this. I'd spent a good portion of the day with him and had been drinking. I find alcohol to be a great aphrodisiac. More time elapsed, and as you would expect, I started responding to his advances. Before long, we headed back to his parent's cottage. As fate would have it, his parents weren't there. Now that I remember, his parents had a very modest cottage. They were not wealthy people.

I kissed Kyle forever, and then he pulled my bikini off. I was totally embarrassed because I had my period. I had a Tampax. He told me to go and take it out. I was very naïve at the time because all I could think about was, *You don't fuck when you have your period.*

Well, that *rule* did not apply to Kyle. I still remember that day vividly. We were on his parents' bed, and we started fucking like crazy. Truth be told, he was a master at it. He would touch you all over, kiss you all over, and nothing put him off, not even the sight of blood. He was wild. During the process, I was still thinking, *C'mon, we can't fuck because I have my period, right?*

Wrong! I learned that absolutely nothing was off-limits. My doubts were soon rectified. While I was contemplating my actions, Kyle was fucking me, kissing, touching my breast, lifting me up, and eventually turning me over. Man, that was quite an experience. I was very excited, and he was very physical.

He turned me over, and of course, by this point, I'd been fucked from behind in my pussy. However, no one had ever tried to fuck me in the ass. But as you might've guessed by now, nothing was off-limits for Kyle, and he became the first person to shove his dick in my ass. It hurt like hell. To make matters worse, he didn't use any lubricant. It was very painful and rough. I didn't like it one bit. Luckily, that was the only time he did that. Obviously, I had a great deal of explaining to do to my local GYN when I got home. Why?

Because I suffered an anal fissure due to the ass-fucking we did. It was terrible and VERY awkward.

In all honesty, I loved being with Kyle. He was so irreverent. However, he was very savvy and good-looking. But all things aside, he was a great lover. He was so spontaneous that we'd literally fuck anywhere, anyway, and anyhow. If I am being completely honest, I enjoyed every moment of it.

I remember a time when we had somehow ended up in Toronto. We were driving north on a Friday, which was, I believe, the Long Island Expressway at that point. We were just creeping along, basking in the sights. And, truth be told, there wasn't much to see. Kyle had a really cute blue Convertible MG. We were bored out of our minds. We were in the sun with the top down, and suddenly he asked, "Give me a blowjob."

Hearing his unusual request, I was like, "Okay. Don't you think people can see us?"

He immediately replied, "Who cares?"

As soon as he said this, I started going down on him and vigorously pursued his wishes. Truth be told, I liked his devil-may-care attitude. He was excited, and I loved the time we spent together. The trucks were honking at us, and Kyle almost ran the car off the highway when he came. It was pretty hysterical.

Sadly, our relationship was coming to an end. There came a time for me to be heading south. At the time, I had a braiding and grooming job with Rock Bottom and at Syracuse International Fair and Horse Show, or whatever it was called. Kyle and I visited my parents for a little while down at the boathouse.

Then, we went for a walk despite clouds of mosquitoes hovering above our heads. My grandfather's driveway was up on a hill. It was asphalt but had a dent in it, along with a grill. As soon as we reached there, Kyle took off his hockey jacket or athletic jacket, whatever you call those jackets, with the leather sleeves and the wool body in the colors of your team. After that, he laid me down and started fucking.

Kyle was very vigorous with the way he taught you and touched you. He also wanted to make you as happy as he could, which of course, he did. He wouldn't touch you too hard. On the contrary, he would play with your pussy and then lick it forever. This was way before the G-Spot was officially recognized, but I swear he would hit it anyway. I would cum like crazy with him. He was nothing short of amazing. Frankly, these were very heady times, and I was going to miss him dearly.

So, coming back, I go to the Syracuse Horse Show, and I'm with my Rock Bottom crew having a grand time. Desmond was off at college and not present there to harass me. This was despite the fact that Desmond never committed anything to me or called me up when we weren't together. Yet still, he was very possessive and didn't want me to be with anybody else. Kyle came down from Canada, which was a sizable drive. It was a good five–six-hour drive, or so, I would guess. This showed that he had put in the effort to see me, unlike some people (Desmond).

Anyway, my friend Amy, who was one of my new best friends, a very wealthy girl with a bunch of horses with

Rock Bottom that I helped take care of, she was showing her horse. She had a room, and there were two beds. Now, she might or might not be there. This meant that Kyle was able to stay with us. Of course, we were on each other instantaneously, and much fun abounded. We were always trying to—not because she would care but tried not to fuck while Amy was present. Now, naturally, there was a little subterfuge to throw some spice and such on things.

In any case, I had to work long hours at the show. On the other hand, Kyle would just hang out, go to the fair, and drink beer. He was Canadian, after all, so his habits came with the territory. I had a great, great long weekend with him. We had always been physically very well-matched.

To be clear, he didn't have a giant cock. This was fine because I was pretty tight. He always made sure I was more than ready. He did things that made me want him desperately and immediately. At the same time, he was not above teasing me. He often pretended that he didn't want me—you know, the games we played. Eventually, we would do battle, and I was always very satisfied with him.

Then, later that fall, I was off to college. However, this couldn't keep us apart for very long. Sometime later, he invited me to his sister's wedding and paid for my airfare, which was fairly expensive in those days. Without a moment's hesitation or second thought, I flew up to Toronto for the wedding.

Kyle was such a rascal. I stayed in the sister's old room or something like that, and he was across the hall. It was a small house. As I mentioned before, his parents were not wealthy. As soon as they would go downstairs in the morning, he'd be running in with a hard cock wanting to fuck me, which of course, I couldn't resist. We'd fuck like we could, and the way we did was truly magnificent. Then, I'd have to go downstairs, and I'd be totally bright red when I had to face his parents.

Before long, the time came, and I attended Kyle's sister's wedding. I'm sure his parents must've thought I was the biggest slut in America and Canada. But frankly, it didn't matter because he and I had fun. I even brought his poster picture to college with me. I remember him fondly.

Quite frankly, my life changed significantly with the death of my dad and being off to various colleges and college experiences. That wasn't going to fit in with Kyle's life, but I've always wished him well and treasured the memory of our sexual exploits. He was great. He was really great!

Years later, he called me, and we had a fun get-together. We talked and reminisced about the old times. I also found out that he was married. I got the impression that he married well and was living in the maritime somewhere, I think it was. We had a good conversation, and it was great talking to him.

Truth be told, I'd love to see him today and fuck him. In fact, I'd be thrilled to meet any of these top-rated studs of mine today and see what we've each learned. If that ever happened, I'm pretty sure we all would've had some pretty interesting, exciting, funny, and awkward stories to tell.

Chapter 6:

Eric Wilson & Ron Franco

My second most pivotal situation came about during the initial stages of my new career. At this time, I met one of the more interesting lovers of my life, Eric Wilson (Eric). Looking back, I guess I had an Eric file at some point. Let me assure you that we certainly don't want to forget him; as I mentioned before, Eric was a rather interesting lover.

Now that I think about it, the circumstances surrounding our first encounter were hilarious. This was an exciting time for me. In fact, this was the beginning of my realization of the sexual power I had as a gorgeous 15-year-old model. I was just starting to explore the world of modeling. It was a whole new world for me, and by this point, I had become accustomed to it. The attention, the idolizing, and the admiration had turned into a routine for me. And truth be told, I loved each and every second of it.

During this time, I gained a power that I'd never had before—the power that beautiful women possess to get away with all sorts of things. I had acquired it, and if I am being completely honest here, I learned to use it as well. In fact, this power even allowed me to get into the good graces of Eric.

Just like everyone else I met, the teachers at my school were starting to follow me around. It was a very large school, and the students could tell that most of the professors had taken a fancy to me. It appeared as if the teachers would do anything to be with me. Don't get me wrong; I was flattered, but not everyone deserved my attention.

In particular, my geometry professor—I hated geometry, loved algebra—was always flirting around and stuff. He had another friend that taught some other subject and was also always flirting around. Both of them tried their level best to gain my attention. They used every trick in the book, but it didn't work. Why? Because my eyes were set on someone else.

Truth be told, I was interested in only one of them, their buddy, Eric. Eric was the boys' gym teacher. He was a gorgeous black-haired beauty with blue eyes. At the same time, Eric was very fit but very shy as well. To be honest, it took him quite a while to pick up on my hints. I practically threw myself at him because there was just something about Eric. I knew that he had the potential to be a great lover; somehow, I knew it. He had this magnetic charm that simply couldn't be ignored. So, as you would've guessed, Eric gained my undivided attention.

One night, I got invited to his apartment along with the other two teachers. It was a nice apartment, very spacious, perfect for partying. It didn't take long for me to get in the mood and let loose.

Yet still, I didn't get distracted. My target was Eric and no one else. I deliberately went toward where he was standing and started a conversation. Initially, he was surprised and reserved, but slowly he opened up and showed his real personality. He was really funny, and surprisingly it turned out that we had a lot of things in common. As always, my hunch was right. Our talk became more intimate by the minute, and we both knew where it was heading. I was really excited.

After talking, kidding around, and maybe having something to drink, in fact, now that I look back, Eric and the other professors might've been trying to ply me with liquor. I don't know; that could've been a real possibility. In any case, I was honestly too drunk to care. Eventually, Eric said, "Come with me."

There was a door across from where we were sitting. It looked like it headed toward a bedroom or something. Eric took me by the hand with a sly glance at his friends and walked me over into what was not a bedroom but a large closet. I was shocked when I saw this because, frankly, I had never seen such a huge closet before. For an apartment that size, the sheer presence of a giant closet was rather weird. However, at that moment, I was too preoccupied to think much of it.

The moment we entered the closet, Eric started kissing me, caressing me, and doing all the right things. We ended up on the floor, rolling around and exploring each other in a passionate and intimate manner. It was very intense, and I believe both of us were performing at optimum capacity.

Then, in the heat of the moment, all of a sudden, Eric asked me, "Will you give me a blowjob?"

In all honesty, I knew what a blowjob was. I wasn't that naïve, as you can probably tell from reading this book thus far, But, at the time, I had no idea how to give one. I didn't know the dynamics of it, and if I didn't know something, I'd always point it out. And that's what I did. I simply told him, "I don't really know how."

He responded enthusiastically, "I'll teach you, no worries. Just follow my lead."

Without a moment's hesitation, I replied gleefully, "Great."

Within a few seconds, Eric whipped out his cock and showed me the basics of sucking cock, licking it, and playing with it. It was not only interesting, but I also found out a rather peculiar thing about myself. I discovered that I really liked giving blowjobs. To be honest, I had missed, age-wise, hand jobs. As a result, I never learned to give a decent hand job, but I could give a great blow job. I could tell from his reaction that he obviously loved it. Seeing his satisfied face, I immediately thought, *Aha, one of the secrets.*

Now, meanwhile, out in the living room, the other teachers were in hysterics. The signal Eric had given them earlier on had revealed everything. So, there was no way we could hide it, even if we wanted to. After we both came, Eric and I sort of put ourselves together and came out of the closet, so to speak. I looked like the cat that ate the canary. The other guests were exceptionally quiet. They knew they had missed something. The entire situation was pretty hysterical. Because naturally, we had to come out of the closet and face these teachers—the same teachers who were very disappointed that they didn't get a chance to be with me. It was quite funny in retrospect.

Eric and I continued to have an on-off physical affair. He was always nervous that someone would find out at school, even after I was off at college and stuff. Sometimes, it would affect his performance because he often got too anxious. He would always say things like, "Man, I hope nobody finds out. It would be quite the scandal, don't you think? I know these people; they are quite the gossipmongers. I hope this stays between the two of us."

I would always hear him out, tell him to calm down, and focus on the task at hand (fucking me). It was very frustrating, but we managed to make it work more or less. I was pretty attracted to him, but the thing that stood out was his coloring. His appearance was magical for me. Why? Because he had basically the same coloring as my father. This was a major turn-on for me, but I didn't realize this until later on. Eric had this striking, almost black hair and piercing blue or green eyes. In other words, he had this black Irish look. It was very sexy, and I was immediately hooked when I saw him.

By the time I was in college, I'd run into Eric at the local bar occasionally. Sometimes, we'd end up together, but it never really developed. He was not sure of himself. The shyness he had, which I honestly thought would blow over eventually, continued to dominate his life. On the other hand, I, by this time, was quite sure of myself and comfortable in my skin. As you can imagine, our relationship wasn't going anywhere, and ultimately, we both called it quits.

Looking back, it was a fun, interesting, and enlightening high school experience that needed to be a part of this book. If it hadn't been for Eric, I wouldn't have figured out just how much I loved giving blow jobs and might not have satisfied the future lovers in my life.

As is so often the case, it's hard to capture all the various amalgams of things that make someone a great lover. This is perhaps the greatest mystery in existence, far more valuable than anomalies like aliens, UFOs, and black holes. Why? Because judging who's a great lover is so relative. It varies from person to person. It's different for who wants what. Some people prefer‍ quickies, while others want foreplay. It is rather complex, and two lovers need to discover it on their own. At the same time, not every lover is going to suit you.

Now, at this point, I've looked at my list of lovers. And, in all honesty, I've probably forgotten some, or I chose to forget some. There are several reasons behind my indifference, but the chief reason is that many of my lovers were mediocre at best. On the other hand, the ones that I'm telling you about in these chapters were the magic men. They were the truly inventive ones, the ones you craved as soon as they left your life.

In my perspective, I believe that's what someone would want to read and hear about. However, I also believe that there's no point in talking down on someone who was your lover just because it didn't work out. It's no one's fault since lovemaking and intimate relationships are very complicated endeavors. However, sometimes, it's someone's fault, and it's nothing to be ashamed of. To this day, I miss Ron Franco and his sweet smile. As you would've guessed, he was also one of the infamous magic men, and you'll learn more about him in this chapter.

In all fairness, Ron was an unusual choice for a lover. Perhaps his greatest quality was that he was super cute. He had carrot-top red hair and freckles. He wore his hair long and had (as I've mentioned before) a great smile. Talking about his job, he was actually the mailman of the town. He loved his job because he'd travel around his route, deliver all the mail, and then he'd have the afternoon off.

And, as you'd expect, he would utilize this free time in the best way possible. Ron would go drinking at the local bar or something. The most surprising thing was that he got away with this for years. He was six foot five, I think, nicely built, and loved to have parties. Every time he had a party, he would call me up and ask me to come. I knew that meant we would be together, which was wonderful, but these parties were so crazy and so much fun. Ron lived in the slums of Orange, New Jersey, but it would be an open house. The place would be jam-packed. We played Motown songs all night, and we'd have line dancing and sing along on a regular basis. As a matter of fact, it was all really the local Montclair crowd at these various stages. In any case, these people knew how to party.

Truth be told, Ron, and I always ended up together. From that first spark when we met, I knew it was going to happen, and eventually, it did. After one of the parties, he was like, "Can you stay for a while?"

I replied very enthusiastically, knowing what he meant, "Sure, absolutely." We were both big drinkers. As a matter of fact, I used to be a heavy drinker during this time. I don't drink a lot anymore, but back then, I would drink a lot. What can I say? I liked to party hard.

In those days, I almost always had to keep up with the boys. I couldn't let them think any less of me. So, I had to be the wildest girl in town. And, sure enough, I was. I had to be able to smoke more pot than anyone. Remember, this was the 60s and 70s, so cocaine played a huge role in my life. By the time cocaine became easily accessible, I would do more cocaine than anybody.

Of course, my brother is not included in this, but of all the other people I knew, I would push myself the most. Let me clarify that I never actually bought cocaine. Most of the time, I didn't even buy marijuana because my brother would give it to me. One time, my Rock Bottom connection had brought hashish over the bridge from Canada in 1970. I loved hashish. It made me lose my inhibitions completely, which, in all honesty, can be really frightening. Yet, the pros far outweighed the dangers. It was truly a fun experience.

So, like always, we were smoking at Ron's home, drinking, as I said, and singing, and dancing. Then, suddenly, Ron brings me upstairs. We started exploring each other sexually and figuring out what the other liked. I discovered that Ron had a truly huge cock.

As I've mentioned in previous chapters, I'm kind of tight, but Ron was just great. He would make sure you were wet as could be and had already cum; then, he'd enter you very gently and gradually. After that, he'd start to fuck you in a meticulous and passionate fashion. I would usually be on top because that allowed me to control stuff. He'd then turn me over, and we'd make love in different positions. Interestingly, Ron loved my small perky breasts, and I loved him touching them along with kissing my neck. He was so fun to kiss, and he liked to kiss.

He had such a sweet smile and huge hands, but he knew how to control them. I used to be pretty sore in the morning. However, let me clarify that every time we fucked, he never hurt me. Ron would wait so long with lots of foreplay until you were desperately craving and wanting him. I would start out on top so I could control the insertion. This was rather interesting because the *Kama Sutra* categorizes lovers by their sizes and which sizes work best together and which don't.

In retrospect, I think Ron was probably too big for me. This meant that I was possibly too small for him.

71

However, despite this, we certainly made it work. We just had so much fun. His hands would just support your entire back. He would move his hips on me, and you could also move your hips on him. To be honest, I never regretted a single time I was with that man.

Everyone knew that if I was at the party, I would be there with Ron. We would dance, do line dances, sing Motown and drink tons of beer and occasionally a shot of whiskey. So, one day, we ended up upstairs, but we were not alone. There was a total of four of us sitting in one of the spare bedrooms that had twin beds. Ron and I were sitting on one bed. Richard and this girl, who I didn't know, but I figured she was from Kimberly, the girls' school, were on the other side. We were all really just facing each other, sort of knee to knee. It was pretty awkward, but I didn't give it much thought. I was a very open person. All of a sudden, this girl starts giving me dagger eyes. I'm looking back at her like thinking, *What the fuck's your problem?*

Then, I noticed a rather peculiar fact. This girl kept on looking at Ron, then me, and I could easily tell that she was under some kind of misapprehension of thinking.

Perhaps, this girl honestly thought she was supposed to be there with Ron and not me. It didn't take long for her to showcase her anger and pettiness. After a few minutes, she said something really snarky to me, which I didn't take too kindly to. I retorted sarcastically, followed up, and said, "You look like you're a Kimberly chick."

She goes, "You look like you're a whore."

At which point, before she even got it completely out of her mouth, I was up and punching the shit out of her. The guys were totally flabbergasted. I like to add that I can throw a mean punch. And, back in those days, I was strong as an ox. I told her what I felt right to her face. I said, "Don't you ever try and talk to me like that again."

I also said furiously, "I'm Ron's guest here." The guys were totally flattened against the walls. They couldn't believe I had done what I had just done. They couldn't believe the ferocity with which I attacked her. After the shock wore off, the boys were in hysterics. She, on the other hand, started crying and ran out of the room. I was like, cool. In my mind, she was a petty bitch and got what she deserved. Truth be told, I didn't lose any nights of sleep thinking about her.

In any case, this was a pretty funny story that I had with Ron. We laughed afterward at the fact that I punched her out, and she thought she was with him. The only other time I got in fisticuffs was at college, and it was well-deserved. This guy was a sex marauder at college who was going around and had a pair of girl's underpants. He would often ask the girls creepily, "Are these yours?"

There was only one dorm with girls, as it was only the second co-ed class at Franklin and Marshall in Lancaster. This was the top pre-med school in the country for college. If you got through here, you could pretty much write your ticket.

At any rate, I was there and doing pretty well. In any case, back to the marauder. Now, in college, we had this little kitchen room. There were three or four of us in there, and you could see straight across to the shower room. I saw this little girl. She had a little stature and thick glasses and was going there with her towel and robe. She was obviously going to take a shower. Then, I saw this weird guy duck into the corner of the room. I walked across the hall, headed inside, and looked. This pervert was staring in the shower the girl was in. I knew I had to do something. This called for immediate action.

Now, college security had warned us about him. Yet still, I walked over there and, in my lowest-pitched voice possible, said, "What are you doing in here?"

He looked at me, and then he realized something. He figured that since I was a girl, I wouldn't be much of a threat. To tell you the truth, I think he simply didn't care. Seeing this, I grabbed him by the shoulder and just started pummeling the shit out of his chin with my left hand while holding on to his collar. He totally freaked out and ran down the hall with me attached, pummeling him into oblivion.

Let me point out that I was really strong in those days. I'd spent my entire life around horses. I was 5' 10" and a half, wiry as hell. In other words, he was no match for me. He did try, though. This pervert was trying to get rid of me, flailing around and running as fast as he could toward the hall. The girls were all flattened against the side of the hall. I let go of him when he ran down the stairs into the park because I felt that I had already sent a clear enough message.

Sometime later, the dean summoned me to his office and explained why I shouldn't have done what I had done. He explained that I could've been hurt blah blah. After listening to him carefully, I simply stated, "What about the little girl in there? Who knows what he was going to do?"

He didn't say anything because he knew I had made a valid point. Then, he told me to go back to my class and instructed me to warn the authorities before I thought of doing anything drastic. So, as you can see, both of my *victims* deserved what they got.

Apart from these two altercations, I think I got into a fight one or two times. Usually, I'd hold myself in a certain way so that people didn't bother me. As a result, I didn't have to deal with a lot of drama and petty squabbles. In fact, I was able to handle myself pretty well.

Anyway, coming back to Ron, this guy made love in all the wonderful ways imaginable. As I reminisce about the time we spent together, I have become even more interested in Ron. I just realized just how much fun he was. I mean, he would do a number on me, that's for sure. But this didn't dampen the spark and passion of our relationship in any way.

In my view, the *Kama Sutra* describes our situation pretty well. Apart from physical compatibility, this fabulous book also talks in vivid detail about the different kinds of love bites one can have in the heat of passion. It describes how wonderful it is to have bite marks that can remind you of your lover and the sex you had. That's kind of how I felt about the time we spent together. No matter what I do, I cannot forget Ron.

Now, if I am being honest, Ron and I didn't have that much in common. Yet, he had been my lover for quite some time. It was always wonderful. I would see him around town occasionally. I don't know what happened to him, but he's definitely someone I would worry about. If given a chance, I would relive the intense moments that we once shared over and over again. That's how good he was, a true magic man.

Chapter 7:

Blowjobs & Definitions

Now is probably a good time to put some context into the definitions of words I use. Because, in all fairness, some of the words I use can have more than one meaning. This can cause a great deal of confusion, so I believe it's best if I clarify any misconceptions that may or may not occur. Trust me; at this point, things are about to get even more interesting. That's why it's in everyone's interest if we stay on the same page. Let's begin.

First of all, we'll start with blow jobs. As I've said before, I love to give blow jobs. I love the power I feel and have over my lover. The moment I start giving a blow job, I know I have my lover's complete focus. I have him in the palm of my hands, both literally and figuratively. And, truth be told, it feels amazing.

At the same time, I love to pleasure a lover that's pleasing me the way I want. This doesn't mean that I prefer my needs over my lover. No, not by a long shot. In fact, my lovers would agree that I am not selfish by any means. If I am into someone, I'm into him with my heart, body, and soul. In other words, I'm willing to do anything to satisfy the other party. So, I pretty much expect the same. And, up till now, most of my lovers have set the bar extremely high.

I have only one simple rule, giving and receiving the best, and I follow it almost religiously. This means that if they're going to go down on me, they're going to get a much better blow job and at much longer durations. In this scenario, it's up to each of us to determine the length of the other's pleasure. Sometimes, I would give blow jobs for several minutes. It all depends on the person I'm with, and I never judge anyone. For me, if he's invested in me, I will be more than happy to return the favor tenfolds.

Now, let me point out that blowjobs can be many things. As a matter of fact, they can be anything from just licking, sucking, holding, and such to sucking a guy off. This was very exciting for me because the person I was with enjoyed what I was doing. The standard process of sucking a guy off was somewhat of a mystery to me. The reason is it became a common process before I started giving blow jobs.

I had to learn it and then practice it. It was fun, but it took some time to master.

In my view, this was quite an achievement because I started doing this as a teenager and college girl. I was only a young model, and having that much experience was not by any means normal. None of my friends had dabbled in this erotic art as intensely as I did. And I'm pretty sure it affected their relationships later on. On the other hand, I can say for a fact that my intensity paid off.

I learned a thing or two about blowjobs from perhaps the greatest lover or love of my life, James. Don't worry; James has his own chapter, which contains all the nitty-gritty details of our time together. Anyway, I recall that one day James brought me to New York City to see the movie *Deep Throat*. I was only seventeen at the time. So, obviously, learning what could be possible in a blow job was a real revelation for me. I couldn't even imagine it because I would gag if I tried anything like that. The way the guy was pummeling his dick into her. It was very surreal for me. I remember thinking, *How is she breathing? How is she not vomiting right now? Is that even possible?*

Years later, I learned from my wonderful lover Phil how to give a deepthroat. He was the one who really encouraged it. Because, as I recall, other lovers were happy with the normal licking and playing around. Phil, on the other hand, had a bigger appetite and far more control. So, as always, I was ready to give him what he wanted.

To be fair, I loved to please him as he pleased me. Phil had such a way with his tongue and fingers that I would start making sounds of pleasure the moment he touched me. So, naturally, I had to return the favor. In fact, I learned so much about deepthroating that I was able to relax my throat and get my neck at the right angle. This allowed me to give a pretty good version of deepthroating, which Phil enjoyed above everything else I was doing. I just loved the look on his face when he came; it was so visceral. It showcased just how much of a good job I'd done. And this was extremely rewarding. That, pretty much along with any combination of caressing, kissing, etc., is how I would describe blow jobs.

I think losing virginity is pretty clear at this point. I don't believe I need to explain just how you lose your virginity, especially at this point in the book. So, without further ado, let's get into fucking. In my perspective, fucking is a very broad term. It can mean casual sex. It can also mean incredibly intense love-making.

What else do you call it? Screwing? Fucking? Fucking is wonderful because it's endless. The sheer possibilities, combinations, and things two lovers can come up with, read, or even think about are extraordinary. As a whole, fucking can fit into numerous categories that lovers can engage in without feeling bored or drained out. In my perspective, it is an entire art that I believe should be taught to everyone regardless of one's culture, religion, or prejudices.

At the same time, kissing can be anything from a peck on the cheek to deep, long tongue-battling kisses, which is something I favor, and anything in between. Kissing can involve the tongue, lips, the breath itself, and other factors which make it all the more rewarding. If you ask me, kisses all over the body are wonderful.

In fact, my favorite lover would be the one who pays a lot of attention to kissing my neck, which is very sensitive. It is a real turn-on for me, and I often wonder why most men aren't aware of this. I also love getting my pussy licked and kissed, and I can't imagine who wouldn't. It's so satisfying. It's almost as if you enter a new dimension. At least, that's how I feel. Every time a guy licks and kisses my pussy, I make sure that he gets the same treatment from my end.

Unfortunately, I am also aware of the fact that not everyone loves sex the way I do, which is quite a shame. People have a fair bit of scruples when it comes to sex. It's very shocking, but that's how it is, and I accepted this a long time ago. Not everyone can be that open-minded, and I get that.

In any case, I will probably think of other things that I have to elaborate on in the near future. But the things I've mentioned above will serve as a start and give the basics. In the coming chapters, I will, for the most part, use fuck to describe sex, blowjobs to describe blowjobs and someone going down on me, going down on me. As I've mentioned before, I am a very generous lover, and there's little I won't reciprocate without getting too far out there.

With fucking, there are so many wonderful positions you can try. The *Kama Sutra* is filled with information regarding what size men and women should be matched together. This amazing book recognizes the fact that not everybody has the same size, depth, or length of cock. This means that the cock size determines what positions you can get in. Not every position is suitable or even possible for some men, and that's completely fine. For me, being involved, intense, and intimate are the factors that matter the most. If a man can do this, he will have my approval on all fronts.

Of course, you can be fucked from the front. You can be fucked from the back. You can also fuck doggy style. With me, it was always—I loved to be put in multiple positions. I loved the man telling me what to do and how he wanted me. So, in a way, it didn't really matter if I was on my back or on my front. Although I did appreciate lots of hand contact, rubbing hands over my body, kissing me everywhere, and showing his pleasure. Because through his feedback, I knew that he was getting what he wanted.

Then, there's also the matter of where you're fucking. I can assure you that atmosphere is a great thing. If you don't have the right ambiance, no matter how good your lover is, you will still feel unsatisfied. He could have a giant cock and be very skilled, but if the atmosphere is not working out, nothing else will. So, before you do the act, always make sure you have the environment of your choosing.

If you were to ask me, I often had trouble if the music was on. It would throw my rhythm off completely and ruin my mood. A lot of times, my lover would say things like, "C'mon, baby, it's just music. How can it be that off-putting? You're exaggerating a tad much, don't you think? How can you not be in the mood all of a sudden?"

And, once I was turned off, I would stay that way for a while. I didn't listen to anyone, and honestly, it became quite frustrating for my lover. However, that's how I was, and I could only do so much. In the end, in my opinion, there's nothing like exploring each other's bodies, going from oral sex to deep kissing to being on your back with your legs up on your lover's shoulders. It's definitely something to experience—an experience that will stay with you forever. Luckily, I had this experience several times in my life, and I am tremendously grateful to all my lovers that made it happen. You guys are the best!

Chapter 8:

Lilly & Modeling

I believe that this is the right time to introduce perhaps the second most important thing in my life next to sex, modeling. Horses go before this. Why am I saying this? Because modeling had such a tremendous impact on my life that I was never the same person again. I had completely transformed for the better, and my whole approach to life had changed. So, as you can imagine, modeling holds a special place in my heart, and it HAS to be a part of this book.

Now that I look back, my modeling career wouldn't have been possible without Lilly. Lilly was my neighbor and also a famous model with the Ford Agency. She had been modeling for the agency for quite some time. In a way, she was the face of the agency and had considerable influence. At the time, I also believed that she was tasked with bringing in new talent.

In any case, I was about to enter this fabulous industry with her help. The first time Lilly noticed my natural talent was when she and her husband were over at my parents' house. Being neighbors, we would often invite Lilly and her husband to barbeques, birthday parties, and other occasions. They were nice people, and my dad had become good friends with Lilly's husband in no time. Whenever they would come over, my dad would challenge him to a game of pool while we were busy talking to Lilly about her career. It was truly an enlightening experience, and slowly I started taking an interest in modeling.

One day, as usual, my dad and Lilly's husband were playing pool in our large front hall, which also had a fireplace. The only difference was that I had grown eight inches the year before. This meant that I had gone from being the shortest kid in my class to the tallest kid in my class. It was a huge transformation—one that grabbed the attention of Lilly instantly.

Prior to this, I was just another teenage, short, awkward girl that had few prospects in the glamor and dating department. But now, all of a sudden, I was 5 foot 10 and a half and weighed 125 pounds. I was also whippet, greyhound-thin. In other words, I had the perfect shape for a model, and Lilly picked up on this fact immediately.

When I got to our living room, where Lilly was sitting, I noticed her looking at me and admiring me for a few minutes. Then, she said, "You could be a model, you know. You have what it takes. I can see it. You have a bright future ahead. I can almost feel it. Why don't we get some pictures taken?"

Quite frankly, I was taken aback by her statement. Why? Because the person I was just a year ago couldn't even imagine that this was a possibility. I couldn't imagine, in my wildest dreams, becoming a model. It was surreal from my perspective. But hearing this from an established and influential model like Lilly, I began to think that I probably had a chance. I agreed with her proposal, and she told me to pack my things as soon as possible. Initially, my dad and mom didn't agree with my career prospects and potential. They believed it was a lost cause, but upon the insistence of myself and Lilly, they gave me the green light. A new journey was about to begin.

After two days, Lilly took me to New York. We went to a friend of my brother's father's photography studio. It was a decent enough professional studio, one in which any aspiring model could showcase her skills and have a real chance. When we got there, Lilly was the one who did my hair, makeup, and clothes.

By the time I was ready, the photographer had told me to come to the shooting room, and he took the pictures. Even from the first polaroids, we could tell that the camera loved me. I'm very photogenic, and with a good photographer, I could literally out-stage anyone. Lilly loved my pictures and told me to be prepared for the next day. I was really excited. Even though Lilly specifically told me to sleep and get some rest for the big day ahead, I was too excited to sleep. I eagerly waited for the next day.

The next morning, Lilly took me to Ford and Wilhelmina, the two top agencies in the world. These two were like the Coca-Cola and Pepsi of the modeling world. This meant that if they sponsored you, you would be set for life. I did my auditions in both these companies and got accepted as a prospective high-fashion model due to my size. Back in the day, models weren't as tall. So, my height became my saving grace, and I had officially begun my new, glamorous career. I did it!

To manage both my studies and career, I started leaving high school at noon, hopping on the bus to New York City, which was only about 20 minutes away at that time of the day. I did this because I had to go to appointments. I couldn't be late; otherwise, I would miss the gig. So, I made it a point to arrive as early as I could. Truth be told, I wasn't taking any chances. I had to become a professional model at all costs.

Looking back, I was on what they called the new board in those days. Lilly felt I was best suited with Ford as Wilhelmina and I photographed remarkably similarly. In Lilly's mind, this was a real problem that could adversely affect my career. So, she suggested sticking with Ford for the foreseeable future. I heeded Lilly's advice and became a regular model for the agency.

Apart from the photography issue, Wilhelmina also had a husband with a roving eye, I'm told. Lilly was probably trying to protect me from this guy, and I have immense respect for her even to this day. My career could've been a rather short one if it hadn't been for Lilly's advice. And for that, I'm eternally grateful.

Some time elapsed, and I became the senior model for Ford. I had been at the agency for quite some time and was engaged in a number of projects. Although I was not especially busy, I was quite successful as what they called an exotic or high-fashion model. This was rather funny because I'm blonde. In all honesty, I was in a certain way exotic but actually very *WASPY. WASP*, if you young people don't know, stands for White Anglo-Saxon Protestant. It signifies those Americans who were upper-class, highly-influential white people tracing their ancestry back to the United Kingdom. In my view, I fell under this category almost comically. In my opinion, I was anything but exotic. But as Lilly and other photographers would point out, I actually had a unique, foreign look. I had long, thick hair. The cameras loved me, so I would get specialty jobs. I was not a catalog model as much as Lilly tried to make me one. It was a great experience overall, and I enjoyed it quite a bit.

Even now, I have wonderful pictures from the time when I modeled. I have kept some of them, but most of my pictures were lost. I have also framed some of the pictures for my ex-husband that were more like art pictures. You know, those kinds of pictures that Avedon or Irving Penn would take. Now, don't worry if you are unable to imagine how I looked in these pictures. For your convenience (and pleasure), I am sharing them in this chapter. Luckily, I was able to scan some of the pictures before they had been framed. Take a look:

As you can see, I was a natural in front of the camera. At one point, I even felt that it was impossible for someone to take a bad picture of me; I am that photogenic. It was almost as if the camera wanted me there, strutting myself for all to see. And, if I'm being honest, I enjoyed every single moment I got to be in front of the camera. The experience was truly otherworldly. I mean, I wouldn't trade it for anything. Through modeling, I was able to come out of my shell and become the person I was always meant to be.

To be honest, modeling had been a great deal for me because I had been such a geeky, insecure kid. I didn't have any confidence or sense of security regarding my looks. I didn't think I was good-looking enough to attract guys and date them. Because of this low self-esteem, I wasn't able to approach the men I liked. It was a very frustrating and confusing time for me, and modeling changed everything. I got to meet lots of people in New York City and gained confidence in my presence. I was no longer the shy, geeky, and awkward girl. On the contrary, now, I was a model that was praised, loved, and admired by every man. It was an amazing turn of events, one that I couldn't have possibly imagined for myself.

At the same time, I developed sexual power as a beautiful young woman. This power was truly profound. Truth be told, this power lets you get away with so many things. Trust me; I know. I've gotten out of multiple situations all because of my charm and sensuality. So, in a sense, I owe it all to modeling. If it hadn't been for my modeling career, I might've never had the escapades, lovers, and sensual experiences I've shared in this book.

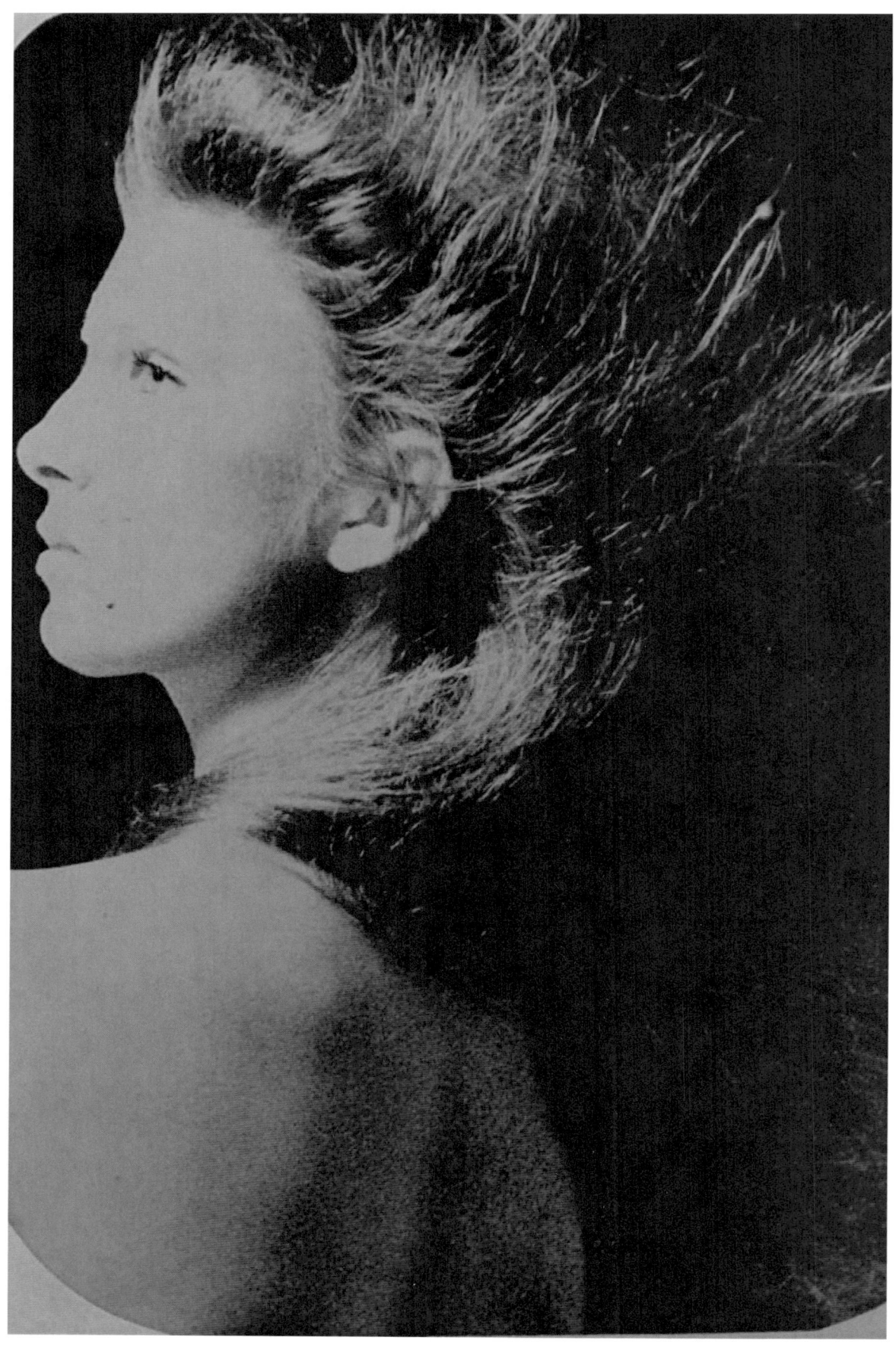

TONY YNO

Chapter 9:

Desmond Perreira

Looking back, I used to spend much of my time as a teenager living at one of my three best friends' houses. It was a really fun experience as I enjoyed their company very much. Their mothers were also very nice to me, perhaps too nice. I honestly believe that their mothers thought I was starving to death. Because whenever I would visit their homes, they would get all my favorite foods in to try and fatten me up. Meanwhile, I'm trying to stay thin for modeling. I really appreciated their gesture of love, but I couldn't tell them the actual reason behind my slim figure. In any case, I enjoyed spending time with them because, in their company, I was able to focus on my modeling career.

Among these three best friends, my closest friend was Dona. She came from a fascinating family, to say the least. Dona's mother was a Broadway and off-Broadway singer, actress, and cabaret singer. This meant that she knew quite a lot of people in the media industry from that time.

Before long, because of Dona's mother, I was exposed to all sorts of exotic New York acting folks. I got to mingle with them quite a bit and received considerable traction for my modeling career because of it. I had the opportunity to network with a diverse group of people—people that had different sexual orientations, ambitions, and unique outlooks on life. They were so open about everything that, in all honesty, you could pour your heart out to them. There were not judgmental at all. And surprisingly, they were very welcoming of new faces in the industry. In a way, I had found my people, and through them, I was able to solidify my presence in the modeling world.

In the horse world, however, I'd already been exposed to many gay men. I didn't really recognize gay women because, quite frankly, this was outside my conceptual framework at that point. In fact, I actually thought that there were more gay men couples as compared to lesbians. As a result, in my mind, the chances of me encountering lesbians were none all the way to slim. I didn't think I'd get to meet a lesbian couple in my life; boy was I wrong. The parties Dona's mother would take me to were filled with lesbian, gay, and bisexual couples enjoying life from moment to moment. It was quite exhilarating, and from that point on, I learned that absolutely nothing was off-limits.

Talking about high school it was a tremendous time for me because I got to discover the big horse shows, which we called the three-day horse shows in those days. At this point, I decided to run away from home and go to the horse show. My friend Carol had a friend visiting, and she'd shown him some of my modeling pictures. This friend of hers was none other than Jack Martin. After Jack saw my modeling pictures at Carol's house, he drove down, agreed to pick me up, and took me to the Monmouth County Horse Show, where he was going.

To be honest, my mother didn't know I was running away. So, I used my mother's huge suitcase to pack for the upcoming trip. The suitcase was navy blue leather. It was beautiful. The suitcase was probably her going-away-to-college luggage set. Jack Martin told me he would reach my home by 1 pm. So, at around 12:30 or so, I snuck out the suitcase onto the front porch.

In half an hour, Jack Martin reached my house in this fancy muscle car. I think it was a convertible Dodge Charger. He was revving his car, and I threw the suitcase in the backseat. Then, I jumped in the car, with my mother screeching at me from the house and running across the lawn toward the car. During her ten-yard dash, she screamed, "Where are you going? What are you doing? Where are you off to? Please, tell me."

I didn't pay any attention to her whatsoever as I had more important things in mind. Within a few seconds, we took off as Jack's engine was already running. Obviously, my mother couldn't catch us as we drove off. It didn't matter because we were off to one of the most pivotal experiences of my life, going to the horse shows. Jack dropped me off at the horse show, and it was there I met Desmond. He was at one of the barns at Rock Bottom. Carol had a friend that she'd gone camping with, Julia.

Julia had told Ann she could get me jobs braiding manes. We braided the manes of show horses with yarn. In most cases, people would sew them in. However, I, on the other hand, was taught to use yarn, which is easier if you want to keep a good quality mane.

So, I arrived at this horse show, and I found Julia at the barn; she worked part-time along with her brother Desmond. It was the top show barn, arguably, in this time period, for hunters and jumpers. Her brother Desmond was tall and wiry, had wire-rimmed glasses, long hair in a ponytail, and was absolutely gorgeous.

Desmond was the barn manager. He flirted with me and also gave me some hashish that he and his best friend, Justin Henderson, had gotten. They had come over the bridge with Canada with backpacks full of hashish. Back in those days, the customs agents were not aware of people doing underhanded stuff like that. As a result, we had tons of hash to smoke, and I loved it. This was despite the fact that I had only gotten high one time prior to this. It was a fun night, and Desmond and I had almost gotten to second base. Eventually, he and Julia hooked me up with braiding jobs, which gave me money. I started to get to know the people at the horse show.

Many decades later, a very famous horseman told me that when he and the other guys at the show met me, they thought that I was the most beautiful woman they had ever seen. The person that told me this is not one to give out compliments lightly. As a result, I was very thrilled to hear it. Yet still, even then, I had trouble believing this. Even though I was doing catwalks and making a name for myself, I didn't believe that I was beautiful. It seemed as if my insecurities still had somewhat of a grip on me. However, it didn't really matter because I had received a compliment from such an extraordinary man.

Meanwhile, his best friend, Mark Dennis, was quite the character, a man that's hard to just put in one box. However, he was a great rider and national champion in what we called the open jumpers back then. Today, they would be called show jumpers or Grand Prix horses. He was always gambling and playing poker.

One year, the guys at first indoors, which are these four international horse shows that I will discuss later, saw him. He was at a sleazy spot at the horse shows. They attacked him; he broke one guy's arm, stuck a pitchfork through another guy, and broke someone's legs. They were never bothered again. It was quite the drama, but I couldn't be bothered with it as sparks started flying the moment I met Desmond. He was very smart; he went to Harvard while his sister went to Vassar.

Julia was Mark's girlfriend. He used to spend a lot of time with his buddies playing poker in one of the tack room stalls, which were horses' stalls where they set up a kind of display room for ribbons, saddles, bridles, and other things. I got to know him and his buddies quite well.

Now that I look, there were a couple of future Olympians that rode the jumpers for Rock Bottom. Joe Fargis, Conrad Homfeld, and a young kid, Anthony D'Ambrosio, were all brilliant riders. Tony Jr. was the youngster of them all and was also very talented. Although the other two were kind of standoffish. They were gay. I don't know if they were together back then, but they were an item later on. At the same time, I got along great with the owners of the farm, Carl and Pat Knee. They also asked me to braid horses, and they liked the work I did. Then, eventually, they asked me to come groom with them.

I loved this because, by this time, Desmond and I had become passionate lovers. It all happened during the first night at the show. During this first night, I had nowhere to stay. I had run away from home but didn't plan it all the way. So, Desmond kindly offered to come to stay in the guy's groom's room. We probably went to the Holiday Inn back in those days. Four of the guys had two double beds. Desmond and I were on the floor. Now, I was very naïve back then. I assumed because these other guys were in the room that, nothing would happen, but Desmond started lovemaking.

He loved to use the word "balling," which, truth be told, I hated. I would often argue with him whenever he used this word. I would say something along the lines of, "That sounds as if the man is in control. This isn't about balling. This is about sex. This is about fucking."

I don't know if I used the word "fuck" as much then as I do now, but frankly, it's the most descriptive thing for this kind of sex. I wasn't about to let anyone consider me the submissive one, even if he was a great lover. For me, like anything else in a relationship, sex was a combined effort.

At any rate, Desmond would go on to seduce and fuck me incredibly. He was a wonderful lover, and we had an affair until he went off to university in the fall. I would go by Rock Bottom, which was in southern New York, a little bit away from where I lived in New Jersey. Usually, I would go and visit, or I would work from there, and we would go to the horse shows together.

In all honesty, Desmond and I would have magical nights out on the grass. This was outside the trailer where the guys lived, and we would make love whenever we got the chance. We would have sex almost on a regular basis on the grass. Desmond would take his clothes off carefully, fold up his wire-rim glasses, put them on his clothes, and usually take the ponytail out. His hair would fall down as soon as he would take the rubber band out, which I found very sexy. He had this beautiful, thick brown hair. We would fuck under the stars. It was quite wonderful. He was very talented sexually, had a great cock, and knew how to pleasure a woman. He was extremely intelligent, so we had great conversations after we fucked each other's brains out.

Later on, in the year when Kyle Singer came down from Canada (the same time I was dating Mike from Canada), Desmond got really snarky with me. He became quite rude to me because I was dating other men. Desmond was showing tantrums despite the fact that he had made no commitments to me whatsoever. In fact, he never called me in the winter, not even once. To be honest, I had no knowledge of what he was doing. I only found out about him through his sister, which whom I, unfortunately, became friends.

Sometime later, I saw Desmond with a girl when I came up to Saratoga for the big horse show there. He was being standoffish with me. He was trying to show that he could go out with other people as well, just like me. Personally, I found this to be rather petty on his part.

In any case, the time I spent with Desmond was one of my favorite times in life; I still miss him. I actually talked to him on the phone about a decade ago. In later chapters, you'll hear more about Julia, Desmond's sister. All that I can tell you now is that she was a complete wacko but who was very instrumental in my being accepted into this new world.

At the time, I considered her a best friend, but her actions in the future would reveal her true character. In fact, now that I look back, I feel that both Desmond and his sister had a lot of issues that I hope they have resolved by this point. I wish nothing but the best for them and remember only the wild, passionate encounters I had with Desmond.

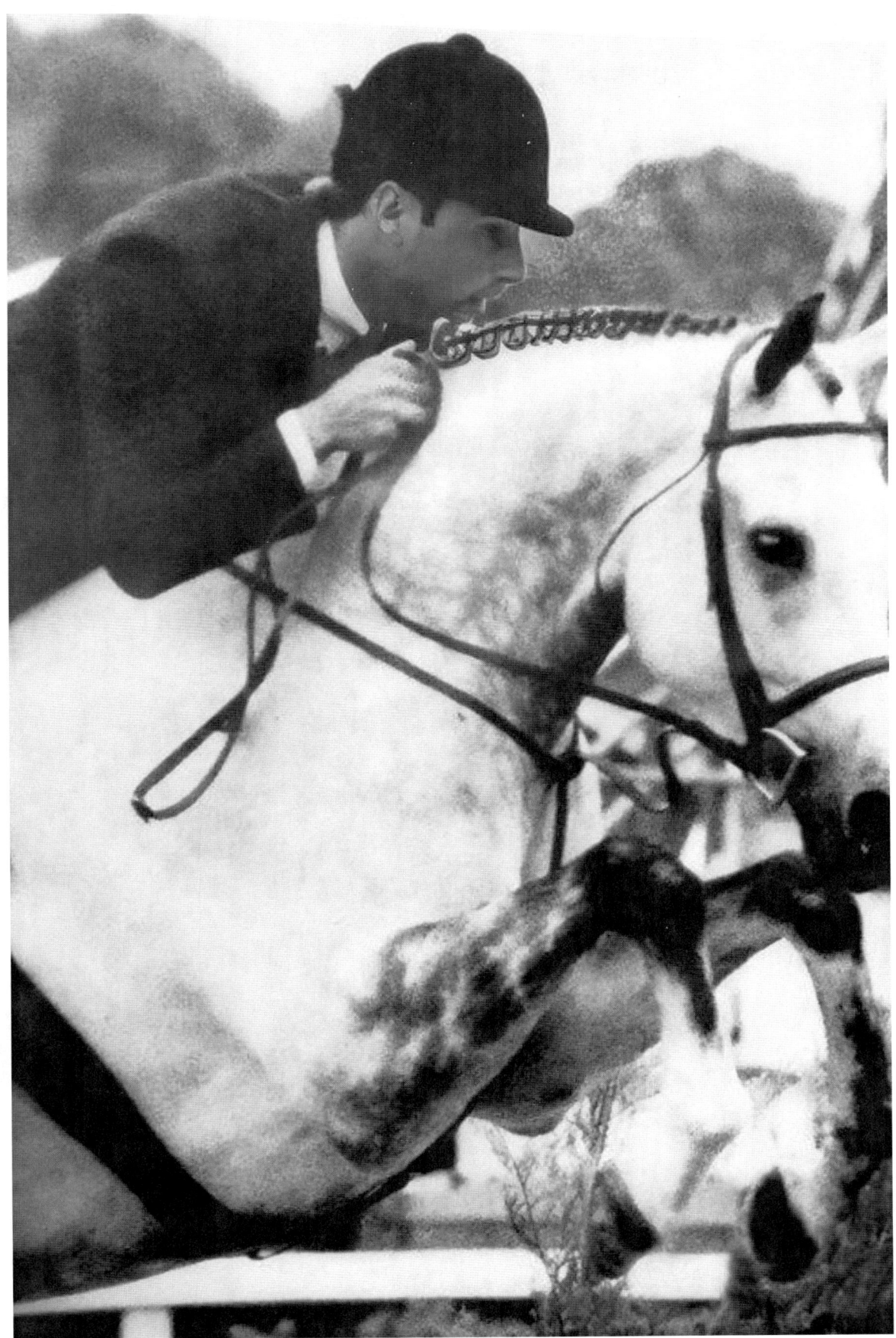

Chapter 10:

Phil's Friend Heath

By this time, the genie was out of the bottle, so to speak. What do I mean by this? I mean that, at this point in my life, I had discovered quite a few sexual techniques. I was no longer a naïve, inexperienced, shy little girl. On the contrary, now, I was a confident dazzling woman who accepted herself and her desires completely. With time, I discovered that I loved sex. At the same time, I also found out that men seemed to love my lovemaking.

In other words, you can say that I had everything working my way. I didn't have any qualms regarding my looks anymore, nor did I feel that I wasn't doing the right thing when it came to sex. I had all the approval I needed, and I was ready to hit the town in a big way. To be honest, it felt really empowering to have this kind of power. I knew that men couldn't resist me, and this meant that they could do anything for me. And, as you'd expect, they did numerous favors for me in my career and personal life. I had so much self-confidence that, for the first time in my life, I felt completely independent. I realized that I could succeed on my own without anyone's support. In other words, I didn't need anyone, and having that feeling was immensely rewarding.

Over time, I developed a series of lovers. Some of these lovers overlapped with others, many lovers became THE lovers of my life, and some affairs lasted seven years. In fact, some of these affairs even lasted decades. So, you can see that some relationships had gotten quite serious. Even though sex was immensely important to me, I was willing to stay committed to the right person. In fact, you can even say I looked forward to these kinds of relationships. And sure enough, I met several men who were decent and boyfriend material.

All the while, I must confess that there were some affairs that were merely perfunctory, one-night stands that didn't really suit me. As a result, I had no interest in prolonging these trysts for a long duration. I couldn't waste my time or energy on these affairs because I already had several suitors waiting for me to give the go-ahead.

Now that I recall, I do remember one black-haired beauty by the name of Heath that would come over to play pool with my dad and my riding teacher. He was not one of those typical, cocky, and arrogant men. As opposed to this, he was pretty decent and had the right looks to boot. As you'd expect, in a pretty short span of time, we became lovers. To be honest, I think my father could tell or suspected that something was going on between us. Because of this, my father purposely stayed up really late, drinking tons of martinis. I was the bartender, so to speak.

Let me point out that my father was quite a drinker. He could drink more martinis than anyone I have ever met. My father had horrendous psoriatic arthritis, which crippled him to the bone. His joints were dislocated, and over 90% of his body was covered with psoriasis. It was really bad and seeing him suffer grieved me beyond belief. I felt so bad that I wasn't able to do anything to ease his pain. To tell the truth, it was an emotionally overwhelming time for me.

The doctors and specialists at Mayo Clinic claimed that it was the worst case they had ever seen. People had this particular kind of ailment, but it didn't progress the way it did in my father's case. In fact, the only reason my father got to know of this disease was through his regular appointments at Mayo Clinic. My father was sent to the clinic every year by his company, 3M. He was a pool shark. They'd had a pool table in the locker room at the Christian Brothers School, where he was a football player.

He was the All-Catholic Quarterback of Massachusetts in 1942 when he was 15. After that, by using fake papers, he joined the Navy and went to World War II to serve in the South Pacific, in charge of navigating an LST. So, naturally, my father was a very tough man, but it seemed like his disease had done him in. In this tumultuous time, Heath served as a glimmer of hope for me, and I grew really fond of him.

One day, my father tried to wait us out so that he could catch us in the act red-handed. Though, my father's efforts had been in vain. Because after some time, due to his ailment, he finally got exhausted and went up to bed. Heath, who was also my riding instructor's college buddy, and I retired to the kitchen. Now let me point out that we had kind of a big kitchen. There was a fireplace there too. Also, there was sort of an L island that stood out.

In other words, this area was the perfect place to screw without anyone figuring out about it. Both Heath and I had the same idea when we spotted that place a while ago. We were merely waiting for my dad to leave. As soon as he left, we started making love passionately. However, much to our discomfort, within the next few minutes, we heard my father walk into the kitchen.

As we'd expected, my father couldn't see us when we were on the floor behind the island. We tried to be as quiet as we could and continued fucking each other's brains out. On the other hand, my father went over to the refrigerator, drank a bunch of orange juice, and then went back to bed. Whether he knew we were there fucking each other or not, frankly, I do not know. However, it was abundantly clear that he did not want to confront us. Now that I look back, my father probably didn't want to lose his pool buddy and baby girl at such a difficult period in his life.

By this time, my parents were starting to adjust to the idea that their little girl was no longer a little girl. They didn't have much control over me because I was an A student. At the same time, I was very bright and had a formidable will, which, as I got older, became even stronger. To be fair, my parents did their best, and they were great friends to me whenever I needed their support.

Talking a bit about my parents, my mother was a kindergarten teacher for 25 years, and my dad ran 3M's largest division, the electrical products division. Because of that, we moved quite a bit in my developing years. To give you an idea, by third grade, me and my family had already moved eight times. This contributed immensely to my shyness early on. However, as I guess you're probably starting to realize, I wasn't all that shy in certain situations, if you catch my drift.

Frankly, it was a very confusing time because some friends of mine were total prudes. While the rest just pretended to be total prudes but were really fucking their boyfriends or having other sexual exploits with their boyfriends. It was total hypocrisy, and for the life of me, I couldn't understand why they portrayed this image in the first place. I, for one, was not the type of person to give in to rules that made no sense to me. I could care less about what people thought of me. So, for me, it was impossible to act prude or anal about sex.

In my perspective, one of the greatest gifts my parents had given me was the understanding that anything a man could do, a woman could do as well. Now, to be clear, they were more concerned with things like education and careers a woman could go in. I don't think they'd ever allowed me to be as promiscuous as the next guy. But regardless, I got to experience and taste the many fruits of life as much as any man. Ever since my early childhood, I always wanted to be an equine vet. Seeing my passion for horses, my parents encouraged me to pursue this career path. This was at a time when some people would snicker and say things like, "Oh, you're a girl; you can't handle those large animals."

But for my parents, that didn't matter at all. Because, after all, they knew I handled horses all the time. I had a horse. I knew I could handle a horse. So, obviously, I was not worried about nursing horses back to health on a daily basis. Later on, I would pursue my passion for a considerable amount of time, but it never quite reached fruition. Yet still, I was happy to have my parents' support and encouragement which allowed me to thrive in other endeavors. If I didn't have their endearing support, I wouldn't be the woman I am today, and for that, I'm eternally grateful.

Chapter 11:

Phil Klang

Oh my, my, I can't believe we've gotten this far without me writing about Phil Klang. Now, I am sure you're wondering why I am saying this. Well, the simple answer is that Phil was probably the greatest fuck I've ever had. Not in all ways, but overall. Phil wouldn't go down on you except under duress. I gave up. I was with him for seven years before I broke it off. There were multiple reasons for this. But first, let me tell you what I mean when I say he was the greatest fuck I've ever had.

Phil was the head property manager for the property management group that handled my cottage. I had known him for a number of years and had arguments with him about various work issues and whether it was done right or not. From the get-go, he knew I could be pretty strong-willed. And I believe this was a major turn-on for him.

He was doing something on my screened porch, maybe doing some painting or something. He's a great painter. At that point, I started complaining to him that I couldn't seem to find any guys in Muskoka. The guys at the club were 80 years old, or they were young family men, and I didn't want to get involved with them at my club.

The following day, I came across his cell number. He was still working on the cottage, and I had felt this craving for him. When I called him, Phil answered with that wonderful, smirky voice. He had recognized that it was me calling, the blond wolf with twinkling bright blue eyes and a husky voice. That Phil, he just had a way of looking at you. It was so intense that a girl had no choice but to feel attracted. Anyway, back to Phil.

As soon as Phil answered my call, he said, "Yes, may I help you?"

His answer told me he was alone. However, I wasn't sure, so I checked this fact by asking him, "May I speak frankly?"

He replied, "I'm alone; say whatever's on your mind."

I responded, "I want you to come up and fuck me."

He said, "I can put that in."

I then asked, "What do you think of me? Pain in the ass, bitch of a customer?"

He responded, "When I was at the cottage yesterday, you said you didn't have enough men to work. I think you need a friend with benefits."

At first, I didn't know what he was talking about. This was a few years ago, back when the saying wasn't that common. Then, I remembered that I had heard about this saying. I knew what it meant. So, I said, "Really? Yeah, you're probably right."

We kidded around about it and stuff, and he didn't come up at the time, claiming that he had to complete the work quickly. He needed to be somewhere. I didn't mind at all because I knew he would be back after the weekends. Why? Because the work at my cottage wasn't finished yet!

To my surprise, the next day, which was a Saturday, guess who showed up at my cottage dock in his boat? You guessed it, Phil. I couldn't be happier. I threw on a semi-transparent polka dot chiffon robe. We hung out for a while.

He'd slept in his boat going to a party. Phil was quite the partier. When I asked what he was doing here, he casually told me that he'd decided to come by. He wasn't fooling anyone. He knew what he was planning. I soon found out he was going to offer to be my friend with benefits, which suited me just fine. Now before we get into the details, I like to point out that Phil was not classically handsome or perfectly built. Despite that, he did have a twinkle in his eye. You could just tell that he was into sex. He had a natural charisma and sex appeal that simply couldn't be ignored.

At the time, I had been quite sick and was quite weak. As a result, we decided to go upstairs to my bedroom, which was beautiful and overlooked the lake and the islands beyond. When we got inside my bedroom, we lay beside one another and started kissing. He was the one who kissed me first, even though he was not particularly into kissing. I guess in the beginning, he made an exception.

When he started touching me and kissing my neck, I told him, "I love my neck kissed." He seemed quite amenable to doing what I wanted. As you probably know by now, I always liked to be on top. So, I got on top of him and rubbed my pussy along his cock, which was substantial. I began rubbing up the shaft across the top, my clit, and then back down. I did this for a while until I couldn't hold myself up any longer. Then, he rolled me over.

By this point, I had cum three times. That's how good the sex was. Being a polite lover, Phil asked me how I was doing. He said, "Have you cum?"

I said, "Yes, three times."

He replied passionately, "Great."

After that, he proceeded to pull me over to the side of the bed. Let me point out that my bed was quite high. It was an antique bed, so reaching that high was a task in itself. However, it did create the perfect angle. He put my legs around his neck, entered me, and started fucking me relentlessly. It was fabulous. To be completely honest, I thought I was going to die. I'm not kidding; Phil was THAT good. I came twice after that. And then, he collapsed next to me. We were really satiated. I remember thinking to myself, *Oh my, I have found a friend with benefits.*

This was the beginning of our affair of seven years, involving every spring, summer, and fall. Normally, Phil would come over after he had instructed his various workmen around the lake on whatever they had to do for that day. Then, he'd come over to my cottage, and we would fuck like crazy. I found out pretty soon that Phil would tell you exactly what he wanted and how he wanted it, which I absolutely loved. Sometimes, I even liked being commanded on what to do. It was a kick for me, and Phil followed through quite well.

We would have sex constantly. It followed a pattern for a while. At the same time, it would get really hot upstairs. He'd be sweating profusely. Because of this, he'd hop in the shower. Then, we'd go at it some more. I was on a bunch of medicines then that made me really horny and multi-orgasmic. It was a trait that I loved, and Phil would constantly test it out.

Phil could fuck forever, so I would cum multiple times. When I couldn't cum again and couldn't take anymore, he'd say, "Are you ready?"

Then, he'd fuck the hell out of me and cum. It was wonderful. Other times, he'd move chairs around and get me in just the position he wanted me in and put pillows around me so I wouldn't feel the burn. We would fuck every time we had the chance. And, it was always combative with us in a wonderful way.

He would sit on my wood stove when it wasn't burning. That way, he could fuck me by placing the chair in a certain position with cushions on the side. He had just the right angle. Quite frankly, I had lost how many times I had cum. He fucked me just like I liked it. I was in my 20s, rock hard and beautiful, so I could have sex as much and as rough as I wanted.

This went on for years, and I always looked forward to seeing him. And by God, he would look forward to seeing me. We would just fuck like rabbits. He taught me how to do deep throat, which I could do a little. Because of Phil, I learned to relax my throat and get to the right angle for deep penetration. I controlled things, and Phil never pushed me too hard. He really fine-tuned deepthroating for me, and I enjoyed doing it every time we had sex.

In other words, you can say that we were carnally compatible to a significant degree. I am sure his boss knew and the local marine guys because his distinctive boat was always docked at my cottage. But then again, there was always work going on at my cottage. So, generally, people had no idea what was really going on.

As I mentioned before, Phil had no problem asking for things he wanted. He wanted to have me from behind. While he would have preferred it if he could have had ass sex, I wasn't into it. It was really messy and painful. I did try it once for him, but I definitely did not like it.

Another peculiar thing was that Phil would watch porn while we would fuck, which, initially, I didn't really like too much. At a certain point, I was like, if it made him happy, I would be happy with it as well. Because, after all, he was making me really happy. In my mind, that's all that matters.

Sometime later, various people found out about our affair. However, in all honesty, I didn't care. I was having fantastic sex frequently during the week. So, I didn't mind the rumors or the gossip. I was more focused on the person that mattered, Phil.

Unfortunately, our relationship died its own death at a certain point. Our fling was very passionate, but I felt that we needed a break from each other. To be honest, after all these years, I still crave him far more than all my other lovers. Oh, those years and that sex un-fucking-believable.

Phil was a man that could fuck you from behind, hold onto your breasts, and not let go of you, and he would even change positions, still not letting go of you. He'd always ask if you were ready and find out if you were ready to cum. If you had already just cum and he didn't notice for whatever reason, he would confirm. In my case, usually, you could easily tell when I came or not.

He was always trading up with different girls in different years. However, I later found out that he finally did commit to a girl. I don't know how long it lasted. Hopefully, they're still together. I wish him the very best.

Lord knows he gave me enough pleasure for ten lovers. I could easily pick out a handful or two guys that didn't work out. However, I wouldn't trade Phil for ten other guys. To be honest, it's hard sometimes to understand how good Phil was. He had an ability. One, he would find the G-spot to beat the band and make you come. Two, he had the ability to direct his cock to the G-spot, up to the top of the vagina, around your cervix, just really—covering your entire genitalia with his hard cock or his rough fingers. It was really masterful, truly educated, and sophisticated cockmanship!

As I mentioned before, he knew I liked to start above him and just rub on him with my pussy, rubbing his cock all over until I came, sometimes more than once. He complied with my wishes at every turn. Then he'd turn me over and fuck me the way he wanted. After that, he'd pull me over to him and start pummeling me with deep, intense strokes. In other words, he would fuck me roundly, soundly, and wonderfully. He just had the knack, and I wish that a vigorous lover like him would cross my path again in the near future.

Chapter 12:

Jeff Dawson

At this stage of the book, I really feel that I need to discuss my first-ever true love. The person I fell head over heels in love with and, at a time, considered my soul mate. This happened during the fall when I was alternating between school, modeling, and running away to the horse shows. My favorite hobby was being at horse shows. As fate would have it, I met my first love at Monmouth County that same year. He was with his cousin Lorenzo. I was introduced to him, and I was instantly smitten with him. There was just something about his personality. He was Jeff Dawson.

I don't remember if we got a hotel room. He was older than I was. He was not that old but definitely more well-versed in the matters of the world. His father was a private jet pilot. Jeff was a mechanic on the planes. It was the time of the Vietnam War, and everybody was trying to be in some necessary occupation to not get drafted. Maybe my old brain will remember that first night vividly, as I'm sure it must have been great. This was followed soon after by equally wonderful times followed closely by much sadness.

At any rate, let me share this experience with you. My best friend Dona and her boyfriend, who was my third best friend's brother, older brother, and Jeff, drove to Canada. I was in Canada for summer vacation with my parents and brother. They came up to where we were. We were on Blueberry Island on Lake Joseph on the Muskoka Lakes in Ontario, Canada, which was two or three hours north of Toronto. I remember standing on a granite outcropping and Jeff coming over, starting to kiss me and touch me. We would walk around the island and talk endlessly about life, the world, and how we were meant to be together.

Quite frankly, at this point, I still didn't know much about Jeff. However, that didn't stop us from sneaking away from my parents, getting in the boat, going to an island, to somewhere quiet, and we would fuck. We were both equally matched.

In all honesty, I don't know what made him so special, but he really was special to me. First of all, the love we had was really puppy-dog love. You know, the ones in fairy tales that involve damsels like Cinderella and Snow White. Jeff was the first lover that I loved, not just loved sexually but also had a mad crush on.

This went on for a considerable amount of time. But, at one point, it came time for Dave and Dona, and Jeff to leave to come back to New Jersey. My parents allowed me to go with them. They weren't coming back for two or three days. They probably gave Jeff and me a lecture that we had to behave ourselves and respect this trust. At any rate, we drove home, all of us having a grand time singing songs and playing the radio in a convertible Lincoln as the Pearson family had the largest Lincoln car dealership in New Jersey.

I got home late. Dave and Dona went home. My friend Carol called me up and said, "Lorenzo Veratti is here. Can I come down with him and Jeff, Lorenzo's cousin?"

I was like, "Great."

They'd come down. We'd do what teenagers do to amuse ourselves. Then, Carol and Lorenzo went to bed in my parents' bedroom as we were not expecting them for two or three days.

Carol was still either lying about what she was doing, and she was fucking Lorenzo, or she was just a cock tease. For me, personally, somewhere along the line, I had gotten it in my head that you never left a guy with blue balls or became a cock tease. Carol was a year younger than I was, and though we were best of friends and had all sorts of misadventures together, she was a very different person in some ways from me. However, we shared other qualities of high intelligence and a privileged lifestyle. I frankly thought my parents had as much money as Carol's parents, but then again, Carol's father was the head of a major New York investment bank.

As a teenager, my house was as big as theirs. I had ten fireplaces. So, as you might've guessed, I did not feel like the poor church mouse. I was a great beauty, which I still find hard to say, though I can logically understand. I have the modeling pictures. I have memories and the things I did, so I don't feel the need to prove it any longer.

In any case, coming back to my first love Jeff, he had what I called the perfect body type. He had broad shoulders, a narrow waist and hips, and a gorgeous ass, and I wanted him desperately. As luck would have it, this was soon arranged, and it was the beginning of a couple of years of us spending time together. He was also a wonderful lover and very considerate. However, our relationship gave me perhaps the most valuable lesson in my life. At this point, I was starting to realize that men lie. They had no qualms about lying about their situation.

More often than not, they would even forget to tell you about girlfriends back home or wives that they have. I was not yet sophisticated enough to have realized this. Jeff Dawson had a girlfriend that he had supposedly broken up with called Elsbeth. Despite the breaking up, he was still semi-attached to her. After we had already spent a great deal of time as lovers, at the show, he told me about her. This revelation completely devastated me. Yet still, it was not a complete deal breaker as he continued to come and see me back in New Jersey, where he was from.

After my initial experience of losing my virginity, learning about blow jobs, and then running away to the horse shows, I had my first oral sex experience with Jeff. I had recently learned to give amazing blow jobs. And, as you'd expect, I happily gave one to Jeff, which he really appreciated. He reciprocated by going down on me, and oh boy, was that great. Talk about making you cum. We started seeing each other on a regular basis from then on.

I, a couple of weeks from then, was going to Canada for our family summer vacation. Jason Pearson was the brother of Shay Pearson, and Shay Pearson was one of my three best friends. I practically lived at their house. They decided they would drive to Canada and come visit me, which was fabulous. Let me point out that I was only 17 at the time. Actually, I think I was 16 then. But it didn't matter because I was deeply enamored by Jeff. There was just something about him. He was a real man's man.

Even though Jeff claimed that he had broken up recently with his long-term girlfriend, Elsbeth, he hadn't really. I don't think so. Initially, he probably just wanted to fuck around, but then he and I started to get really, very close.

That night, after singing along and enjoying ourselves, we got back to my house and dropped off Dona and David. Carol and Lorenzo retired to my parents' bedroom. What they did, I don't know because with Carol, you never quite knew if she was going to tell you the truth.

Jeff and I were in my bedroom, in my antique bed, which was between a twin and full-size. We made love all night, sweating in the August heat with no air conditioning in our house. I wish I could really capture what it was that had me so enthralled with Jeff. I had been with other men. I thought I was very experienced, but of course, I was very naïve.

My dad always was such a man's man. He always felt he could speak to these guys, and they would leave me alone. This was not always true. The next thing I knew, suddenly, in the middle of the night, close to dawn, my father opened my bedroom door and said, "Who is in our bedroom?"

I said something along the lines of, "Carol and her boyfriend." I'm completely naked, covered with sweat and sex.

My father said, "Come out to the upstairs hall." This was the same place we had the piano. I grabbed the first nightshirt I could find without turning on the lights. Then, I walked out into the hall, and my parents looked at me, and I realized I'd grabbed an old nightshirt.

It was a Snoopy Charlie Brown nightshirt that said, "Happiness is Having Friends to Spend the Night." As you can imagine, this was not a good message to come out with. Carol and Lorenzo almost jumped out the second-story window as he was too afraid of my father. Jeff convinced him not to, or Carol did.

My parents thought I knew what I was doing, so they felt very disappointed. At any rate, Jeff skulked out of there. He was embarrassed. My parents were furious at me. They grounded me for a month, not because of them catching us in the act or anything like that, supposedly, but because I had lied to them and not told them—I had told them that I would not be with anyone when I got home. Yet, there we were. He said he was going back to Elsbeth. He claimed that he couldn't face my father again. That, of course, fueled my being even more furious with my parents.

For the next month, I played the song *Lay Lady Lay* by Bob Dylan from Nashville skyline nonstop on my rickety little phonograph blasting from the second floor out the window to the pool and the backyard, which I'm sure annoyed the fucking hell out of my parents. By this time, they weren't quite sure what to do with me. They actually ended up sending me to Canada to spend a month with my aunt and uncle and see if they could civilize me, which I only got in more trouble there. Another tale that I will discuss later.

I, a year later, to the day really, saw Jeff again with his cousin Lorenzo and Carol at the Monmouth Horse Show. I wanted him so badly. A friend of mine's mother was away, and the house was free. She was grooming at the horse show. She offered the house to me, which was great. Jeff and I went there and kept each other up all night. Jeff would kiss your neck. He had a wonderful way of strongly holding you. We would roll around on the bed. At the same time, he was also very good at not disengaging. As you probably know by now, I loved sex beyond imagination, and I was always willing to explore. Jeff was the perfect person to experiment with.

Now that I look back, he felt guilty about Elsbeth and the situation at my house. He lived close to an hour from my house. To tell you the truth, I think he was still with Elsbeth.

My friend's mother was going to be coming back, so we were going to lose the house eventually. At the same time, he was still concerned about my parents and wasn't willing to take the next step. In any case, I will always remember him with extreme fondness, as he truly was my first love. Even though I would've liked our relationship to last longer, I still can't talk badly of him. I wish the best for him and hope that we can rekindle our lost love in the future.

Chapter 13:

Darby Vanderbilt

Now, I will talk about one of the more interesting lovers of my life. You know, the kind of lovers that, even if you don't spend a lot of time with, you simply cannot forget. For me, Darby was that type of lover, and I am excited to share the intricate details of our relationship.

If I were to sum up my relationship with Darby in one word, that word would be "magical." The time we spent together was really magical as I got to experience something new at each turn. It all started when I met someone at school, at Mills, that rode horses.

We met in chemistry class. We were doing some tests, and this person was immediately impressed. I had this persona in which people were instantly attracted to me. So, as you can imagine, I didn't face that much of an issue in making new friends. This girl invited me to her barn once we started talking. She invited me after realizing just how much

I knew about horses and the horse world. Being an equine enthusiast herself, we hit it off and became rather close.

After class, we went to her barn, and I became acquainted with her various horses. In fact, sometime later, I even went to some horse shows with her. We became rather good friends, and later on, she would invite me up to her stepmother and father's place at St. Helena in Wine County. Their names were Isaiah and Jane, and she called them Isaiah and Jane. As I would later find out, this was actually an allusion back to where the family fortune had come from, Isaiah and Jane.

Both Isaiah and Jane were moving back to Southampton, New York. They'd bought a large house which they wanted to restore and fix up. As I remember, it was only a block away from the beach. They took a shine to me instantly and insisted that I come back later on and stay there. They even offered me work on one of the old cottages on the property. This sounded good to me because, frankly, I had nothing planned for the time between college ending and work.

Truth be told, I really didn't have a clue what I was going to do. So, obviously, this was a great opportunity for me to learn the ropes. Plus, being in Southampton Village, which was a very upscale town with beautiful architecture right there at the beach, was a win-win situation for me. At the same time, both Isaiah and Jane were very social and involved in all of the charity events at the art museum. This meant that I could mingle with prominent people in the city and establish my network circle. During these social gatherings, the kids would tag along with us as well. It was Carola, her beau, myself, and then her little sister who would also come with us to the parties. Since she was very young, sometimes she couldn't go to places we could sneak into.

Looking back, Carola was very beautiful, had this great blond hair, and I believe, a little bit of that field hockey girl look in her figure. She worked really hard on herself. She was very interested in my modeling career, which I had let languish. She and I actually had a lot of fun getting her involved in modeling. However, as soon as Carola got in, she became very successful as a commercial model. She was doing commercials left, right, and center. In fact, I think, at one point, she had over five commercials on during the Olympics. This was a great achievement for any model, and I was really happy about her success.

During this time, there were a bunch of kids that kind of palled around. Among these kids, I immediately zeroed in on Darby. To be honest, Darby looked nothing short of a Greek god. He had this blond, curly hair, a golden tan, piercing, intelligent blue eyes, and a wiry body. He was also tall but not super tall. In other words, he had the perfect figure overall, and I couldn't wait to be with him. Eventually, Darby and I started verbally sparring and teasing each other, going back and forth. It was a typical form of flirtation, and it worked. Truth be told, it didn't take long for us to become lovers. In all honesty, I don't remember the exact night or exactly what happened between us.

However, I do recall one night in particular when we were in the kitchen of this giant old mansion that Isaiah and Jane were fixing up. Darby was kissing me, biting my neck, and he ended up giving me a great big hickey. As our passionate encounter ensued, Darby managed to make me cum.

Now let me point out here that there have only been a few instances in which I've cum from being kissed on the neck. In fact, before I met Darby, I didn't even think this was a real possibility, but it was. Darby made it happen. Darby had to hold me up because I was about to fall to the floor. The coast was not yet clear for us to proceed fucking in the kitchen. As a result, we headed toward either the pool or the garage, the grass or somewhere, made love, screwed, and fucked. We did everything we could think of. We were so well-matched that I literally came at least twice whenever we fucked. We fed off of each other's energies, and it was a truly, wonderful experience.

If I'm being honest, the rest of the summer was spent largely with Darby. However, there was something weird I had to deal with. I would never know when I'd see him. I'd run into him at the parties. Sometimes, he'd want to get together; other times, he wouldn't. Now that I look back, I think he loved to keep me off base. To be honest, I was never quite sure what to expect from him. Yet still, I adored him both physically and aesthetically.

Sadly, the summer was coming to a close. This meant that I had to move home with my mother and figure out what I needed to do. Whenever I asked Darby what he was going to do with his life, he always said that he would become a rock star. Seeing his passion for music, I thought I might take up modeling a little bit again. Unfortunately, this was the last time I saw Darby, but what a night it was.

I was in what was probably a maid's room, up the backstairs from the kitchen. I have a tendency to be very messy. So, as you would've guessed, the room was a complete mess. My mother was coming to pick me up in the morning. I was supposed to pack, clean up the room, do all the chores required of me, and right then, Darby contacted me.

As I mentioned before, he was very elusive, and I only heard from him when he wanted to reveal himself. As expected, it was another one of those calls where he wanted to meet. I had no willpower, so I said to him, "Great."

In a short while, he came over to the house. This was a pretty big old house, so the rooms were pretty far apart. As a result, I figured that Isaiah and Jane couldn't hear us. I certainly hoped they did not, but we were loud. We fucked, standing up, from behind, lying down, me on top, you name it. We covered everything we could think of because we knew it was our last night. Darby always gave great head. I did my best, and he was, like all the men I encountered, very pleased. Then, as we cuddled up next to each other, I foolishly said, "I'll drive you home."

I started driving him home in Carola's sister's rattletrap old Volvo, probably waking everybody up. Of course, then I overslept, and my mother arrived, and we probably had a huge discussion regarding how badly behaved I was. I don't believe Isaiah and Jane ever forgave me. This was quite a shame because I thought they were super cool. I learned a lot from them.

In retrospect, Isaiah and Jane did have one good use for me during the summer. The gentleman they had bought their house from in Southampton turned out to be my grandfather's brother. This was the same brother my grandfather had not spoken to since they were children. He had disowned that side of the family and lived with his grandmother, who was a teetotaler. In other words, all the family money went to Uncle Allen. This meant that my grandfather made or married into his fortune. He received nothing from his side of the family.

One day, Isaiah and Jane invited my uncle over for dinner with his wife. They had built this big French provincial house across the lake. They introduced me and said, "This is your niece, Isadora Kelly."

I can still remember the look on his face quite vividly. Uncle Allen was completely flummoxed when he heard this. He was not at all expecting me to turn up all of a sudden. On the contrary, he was originally there to discuss the fact that he had taken the refrigerators, some of the other appliances, and various other things that were supposed to be left behind at the estate when they bought it. They greatly enjoyed putting him on his hindquarters and making him realize that their house guest was his relative. My aunt had kept in contact with him and his daughters, but we never had. It was quite amusing.

Another attractive thing about Darby was that he had beautiful hands and long fingers. He was a drummer. He didn't have particularly large hands, but I never subscribed to the theory that large hands meant large cocks. In my perspective, it's more the actual shape that really matters.

Someone that had long fingers probably had a large cock. If they've got really big hands or fingers, they probably had a large cock, but it didn't make a world of difference to me. Frankly, I don't really care that much about super big cocks. To be honest, they are way harder to manage. You have to make sure you're completely ready before you can fuck them. At the same time, in the case of big cocks, you're more apt to get sore. Or maybe that's just me. In any case, I was not that fond of giant cocks. For me, the lover and the passion he had was a major turn-on.

After that eventful night, I did see Darby on TV once. This was probably 10 or 15 years afterward. He was playing in a reggae band, which I found to be rather amazing. Why? Because we used to have arguments about reggae music in which he claimed that it wasn't great music. But I guess time changes everyone and everything. Unfortunately, he had lost some of his hair, but he was still cute. Boy, it brought back some great memories.

Darby and I would consistently bait each other early on in our lovemaking. I asked him how good I was. I often said something along the lines of, "Am I the best fuck you've ever had?"

He responded, "Probably second."

Then, I proceeded to punch him. The summer went along, and I didn't ask him again. However, the last night we spent together, he turned to me and said, "You probably are the best fuck I've ever had."

This, of course, was a tremendous achievement for me and made me enormously happy. In my view, this was a fantastic way to finish the summer. One could even say this was another summer of lust. In these encounters, you had the opportunity of getting to know that person and what really turns them on. Now, let me clarify that I am not equating this encounter with the first level of lovemaking— the level in which you show off what you found from the experience your lovers liked. No, not in the least bit.

What I am referring to are those intimate moments, such as what parts of their body they are in touch with, that reveal a great deal about your lover. In my experience, most men are basically cock-oriented. They are always turned on by the girl sucking their cock and fucking it as hard as possible. Now, that is all well and good, but, in my opinion, it is fun to expand what may be men's bread and butter.

I, for one, greatly appreciate my lovers trying new things. I love to be told what to do. It's fun. It gives you the sense that you're pleasuring and pleasing your lover. At the same time, you may learn new things or try old tricks that may not have appealed to a lover previously. With a new lover, you can attempt a new variation on a basic theme or a particular type of lovemaking skill or lust. In fact, there are many different levels of pleasure and lovemaking.

In the case of Darby and I, we were truly suited to be combatants in the art of love. Given his elevated hometown boy of high social status, Darby became the king of our group. On the other hand, I was brilliant, somewhat shy, or snotty, depending on how I was perceived by someone. Perhaps they could tell that I was a model, older by a bit.

In retrospect, Darby and I had what I've found common in certain men. The men I had in my life had a desire to be with me, wanting me physically, but did not want to be my boyfriend. Frankly, this was baffling for me. Maybe it had something to do with the way I presented myself. Normally, I tend to be very assertive and strong-willed. Perhaps men find this rather threatening; who knows?

In any case, the overall tension in our relationship and never being quite sure what Darby was up to did keep me off balance. The time we would spend together was always very intense. Moreover, we would only meet after undergoing a lot of planning and discussion on where we would meet when we would meet, and where we would go fuck.

At the same time, Darby and I were both vocal and noisy. We usually tried to go to the cottage on the property, the lawn, the pool, be under the stars or go to the beach. We had a great time romping in the Elysian Fields of Southampton in the late '70s. I wish him all the best and reminisce about the days we spent in that old house, screwing each other without a care in the world.

Chapter 14:

Ben Baker

This is the moment where I introduce you to Ben Baker. Oh, what a time we had together. Ben was not your typical type of lover. No, not in the least bit. He was different, and he made sure that you felt special. That is perhaps the reason why I remember him so fondly, even after all these years.

In fact, now that I look back, I didn't get a chance to spend a lot of time with him. This wasn't because I didn't want to be with him. No, far from it. Actually, there was a geographic obstacle we needed to deal with. Ben lived down in the Carolinas, so coming over to my place was a challenge in itself.

At the same time, we had to decide on these locations beforehand. Otherwise, we would end up in completely different places, trying to locate one another. After we'd finally met and satisfied one another fully, Ben would return to his parents' house.

Ben's parents lived across from one of my best friends. You know, the three best friends I mentioned in the previous chapter. I was very close friends with his brother.

One day, when I was visiting Ben's brother, I met him in person. Truth be told, I was immediately interested in him. The reason was that Ben was exactly my type. He had everything that I found interesting in a man. Ben had that cocky swagger, beautiful body, broad shoulders, thin waist, and of course, a gorgeous ass.

In other words, he was the complete package. There was nothing lacking about Ben. In my perspective, you couldn't possibly look at Ben and not become infatuated with him. That's how attractive he was. And interestingly enough, this wasn't the only thing that made Ben attractive.

Apart from Ben's good looks and impeccable shape, his personality was also very appealing. He was very funny, adventurous, and wild. He was so full of life that you couldn't possibly be bored in his presence. He would kid around, flirt, and talk almost effortlessly. Without a doubt, Ben was a charismatic guy, and I absolutely loved being with him.

Now, obviously, we had to be very secretive about our relationship. I was a close friend of his brother, after all. The situation could get awkward and hairy rather quickly. As a result, we needed to be hush-hush. However, if I am being honest, we were probably not very good at it. I'm pretty sure people found out about our affair. Even if they didn't confront us directly, I'm pretty sure somebody knew what was happening.

In most cases, we would go over to my friend's house when the coast was clear. As soon as we entered my friend's home, Ben would grab my arm and take me to the swimming pool in the backyard. Now let me point out that my friend's swimming pool was huge. I mean, it could fit 10 to 20 people easily. There was more than enough room to adjust and position oneself. So, truth be told, we didn't face any problems with fucking in the swimming pool. And besides, Ben knew exactly what to do. He just had a knack for fucking that I admired a lot. He always made sure I was wet and ready. He wasn't like the random guy penetrating a girl as soon as he touched her.

On the contrary, Ben was an exquisite lover who spent a decent amount of time in foreplay. Boy was that satisfying. Other than foreplay, Ben would suck my breast and kiss my neck. The way he kissed was so intense that I would almost cum right there and then. That's right; Ben is one of the few men in my life who made me cumby kissing me on the neck. As our lovemaking intensified, we would have long, deep, wonderful kisses. Now that I look back, we were pretty evenly matched. Ben didn't fall short in any way, and I made it a point to satisfy him as much as possible. It was truly amazing. We'd be out under the stars fucking and having a wonderful time.

Then, after a while, he would tell me that he had to leave. Ben would have to go home where he lived. I wouldn't see him until the next holiday or whatever. I was usually free, especially for him. I loved being with him.

However, yet again, I would be forced to realize just how true the statement "men lie" really is. Why? Because after some time, I found out that Ben had a girlfriend who, lived somewhere in the Carolinas. He didn't mention her to me or how serious they were. It was as if she had never even existed. Boy, how men can lie through their teeth!

Sometime later, Ben's brother got pissed off, and probably his parents too. They knew he was up to no good with me. And to be fair, it wasn't really my fault. If it was anyone's fault, it was Ben's. He was the one two-timing his girlfriend. I had no earthly idea that she even existed. As far as I was concerned, Ben was mine. And, in the end, it was actually Ben's decision. He was the one that was actually being bad. Oh, he could be bad. He could be so wonderfully bad.

To be honest, I would have loved him to be around a lot. He definitely would have made the hit parade if I could have seen him more. This was mainly because there was only a limited number of times that we'd be together. I don't know. I mean, I would only see him on Christmas, Easter, sometime in the summer, and a couple of times on Labor Day. In other words, I would get to see him only on the holidays. Our relationship was on and off. And, we'd run off and get into trouble somehow, somewhere. It was great.

With time, his family caught on and didn't approve because they knew about the girlfriend. As a matter of fact, the only reason I found out about the girlfriend was through his brother. It was a wonderful experience while it lasted.

The great thing about Ben was that he'd make sure you were especially wet when he'd slide you onto his cock. He had a wonderful cock, not too big, not too small, just the way I liked it. At the same time, the way he used it was so delightful. Now, I'm sure you're wondering, what do I mean by this? Well, to put it simply, Ben could position his cock wherever he aimed. Every time we fucked, he was always very hard. In retrospect, Ben was a very horny guy in all the best ways.

I wish I had been able to spend more time with him as we were very much alike and liked each other a lot. Though, in some cases, geography and various societal pressures destroy a meaningful relationship. Sometimes, the toxicity of other people can become simply too overbearing. It was too much for us, and regretfully we had to call it quits. Oh, what a time it was.

Some things just can't be denied. Among these situations was the attraction between Ben and myself. We were like magnets pulling on each other relentlessly. We even liked the same ways of making love. We lusted for one another. What's more, we weren't shy about where we could kiss, touch, or fuck. I do miss him, though. I hope he's well, and I wish him all the happiness in the world. Ben, until we meet again!

Chapter 15:

Fun Times with Shelly & Rosemary

I'm so excited to share the experiences I had with two of my closest friends. Ever since I started writing this book, I knew that there had to be a chapter on Shelly Billows and Rosemary Bode. Why did I want this? Because the time we shared was truly irreplaceable. Even if I wanted to, I couldn't possibly forget our little antics and shenanigans. They were just so much fun. Oh, what a time we had together. In any case, I won't keep you in suspense any longer.

Shelly was this English girl groom that ran Shane's operation. Shane had imported her along with horses from England. Now, I know what you're thinking. You probably think that Shane did this because Shelly was just another pretty face. Well, let me assure you that this is not the case. Shelly was very good at her work, and Shane knew this. That's why he wanted her to come to the US and take care of his horses. And sure enough, Shelly lived up to her expectations.

Back in those days, she was just a groom. She and I became pals rather quickly. She was a very likable person—the kind of person who didn't pass judgments right, left, and center. On the contrary, Shelly had a clear heart and was always seeking adventure. In other words, she was my kind of girl, looking for bigger and better things.

One day, we decided to go visit our friend Rosemary. Rosemary was originally Shelly's friend. In fact, I only met him when she came to visit Shelly one morning. Both Shelly and I were grooming the horses. However, as soon as I met Rosemary, we hit it off. She was a very cool girl that was willing to help anyone with anything. You could really depend on Rosemary, and she'd never disappoint.

At the same time, Rosemary was such a lively person that she could bring life to any conversation or event. People just loved being around her. So did we. That's why we thought of visiting her in the evening.

Eventually, Shelly and I prepared ourselves, got into my mother's Firebird, and drove down to Rosemary's home. It was a pretty long drive, so we had an ample amount of time to talk. Usually, we would discuss the horses in the barn because we absolutely loved them. We discussed how much in shape the horses were and which one of them had the potential to win the next tournament.

Other than that, we also talked about our lives and what our future would entail. It was quite refreshing, to say the least. By the time we reached Rosemary's home, we immediately headed to the guestroom to enjoy our mutual hobby—smoking pot and drinking. We all loved pot and hashish. Also, we loved drinking tequila, and normally we'd stay up pretty late drinking like a fish. It was really fun. On that day, I think we had close to 20 tequila shots and almost two bags of hashish. As always, we were having a grand time.

As the evening progressed and we became absolutely stoned out of our minds, I think one of us decided it was getting late. I believe it was around 11 pm, and we had to hurry back because Shelly needed to get back to the barn before dawn. Within a few minutes, Shelly and I washed our faces, grabbed our things, and made our way to my mother's Firebird. We got in and left for the barn.

I remember being totally wasted. Now, let me remind you that this happened way before any awareness about mothers against drunk driving or anything of the sort. Back then, if you could drive, you'd drive. As fate would have it, I was able to drive, so I made a long way back home.

Looking back, I was driving pretty well, considering that I was completely toasted. This was quite an achievement if you'd ask me. Everything appeared to be fine except for one rather important fact. I couldn't tell how fast I was going. So, you can say we were in a bit of a situation. Thankfully, I had Shelly in the passenger seat, repeatedly calling out how fast I was speeding. I remember we were on a little backroad highway. You know, one of those two-lane highways which are rather famous in Eastern Pennsylvania.

We had about an hour's drive to get back to New Hope. Throughout the journey, Shelly called out the speed limit to me. Well, frankly, Shelly was telling me the speed I was going relative to the speed limit. Luckily for both of us, it was a slow speed limit. Right then, all of a sudden, I felt something churning up in my stomach. I immediately said, "I got to stop. I'm going to puke."

I stopped the car because I had pulled up on somebody's lawn. As I got out, Shelly also followed suit, and then I puked my brains out outside the car. I had puked everything we had for dinner. Then, Shelly and I both fell asleep, or I should probably say passed out. We had no earthly idea how long we were asleep. It could've been an hour, at least.

After a while, upon regaining consciousness, I remember hearing a car door being shut. As soon as I became aware, I immediately sat bolt upright. When I looked in my rearview mirror, I found out that it was a policeman. Now, I was not sure whether he was a state trooper or a local policeman. But frankly, it didn't really matter; we were in trouble.

Within a few seconds, he came by my mom's Firebird and instructed me to roll down the window. As instructed, I rolled the window down and put on the best, prettiest smile I could muster. Then I asked him, "Is there anything wrong, officer?"

No, as a matter of fact, I first said, "We were tired, so we pulled over to take a nap."

After listening carefully to what I had to say, he replied, "Well, there's actually a good spot to pull over up above where you are now because you're on somebody's lawn."

I responded instantly, "Okay, I didn't notice that. I'm so sorry. My friend and I will get off the lawn immediately. Thank you for pointing this out, Officer."

Then, I proceeded to roll up my window and said, "Shelly, I can't see."

What happened was that when I puked, I had my glasses on. As a result, my glasses fell off in the puke. At this point, we could do nothing but sit there and wait for this cop to pass his judgment. Luckily, the policeman didn't argue that much and left a few minutes after asking some standard questions.

The moment he left, I stepped out of the car in an attempt to find my glasses. It took a while, but I eventually stumbled upon them. They were outside the car, so thankfully, I could see again. At the same time, I was now wide awake. Shelly no longer had to call out the speed limit to me, as I could now function within my senses.

In the next half hour, we finally returned to New Hope. This was one hell of a story, so we kept on laughing at it for the next month or so. It was pretty hysterical, but I am glad I had that moment with Shelly and Rosemary. I would rank it as one of the great tales of camaraderie and fun with Rosemary and Shelly. I hope that wherever Rosemary and Shelly are, they are happy and are having as much fun remembering this tale as I am.

Chapter 16:

An Interlude - Neil Dennis

I think, at this point, an interlude is absolutely necessary. We've already discussed so much in the previous chapters that, to be honest, we needed a break. So, in this chapter, we will talk more about the short vacations I took back in the day. In fact, I believe now is the perfect time to share one escapade I had in Florida.

I was in Florida for the horse shows. Florida, being a very hot and coastal state, allowed me to see things a bit differently. Instead of focusing so much on the horse shows and horses in general, I thought of taking up another sport— the sport which was better suited to my immediate environment.

Eventually, I decided that I was going to take up tennis. In my mind, tennis would be the perfect way to not only enjoy myself but also keep busy. As a result, I wasted no time in arranging a tennis lesson at Palm Beach Polo. I chose this club because of its reputation. Even now, it is one of the most prestigious and premier clubs in the US.

So, naturally, I figured that it was best to learn tennis from Palm Beach Polo. And as always, I made the right decision. I went over there and had a lot of fun. Not only was the club exquisite, but as it turned out, my tennis instructor was also very young, cute, and blond. His name was Neil, but we will call him Neil Dennis.

Neil had been on the cover of *Surfer Magazine*. However, he switched from surfing because of a knee injury to tennis. Even now, for me, it is very hard to imagine that tennis is easier on your knees than surfing. For the life of me, I can't fathom this fact. But as I would later find out, tennis is way better for the knees, or I could have that mixed up. Who knows? There are plenty of things people like to keep a secret. I'm sure Neil had his reasons for leaving surfing.

In any case, we had fun. In my perspective, he was the perfect tennis coach. He genuinely wanted me to learn tennis quickly and efficiently. That's why he didn't stop playing with me after a few sets. On the contrary, we played practically the whole day until it got dark. I had ridden my bicycle over to the club.

For obvious reasons, I didn't have my car available to me. So, I figured a bike would be the right choice. Plus, Florida had all the big lighted sidewalks and stuff. This made riding to the club all the more enjoyable.

At the same time, it wasn't a problem for me to ride back home. In fact, it would be better if I went back home on my own. Yet still, Neil offered to take me home. He had this beautiful black Lincoln, and I was more than happy to go back home with him. I'm sure we both realized where this was going. And, we were kind of enabling it. In any case, things were about to get very interesting.

Eventually, we got back to my house, which was a mess. I had just moved in and hadn't finished unpacking yet. In fact, there was something still there from the people who had lived before. It was very cluttered, and it didn't give off the right impression.

Despite this, I could see that Neil was smitten with me. As we sat in the living room, he grabbed my hand and asked if he could kiss me. Without a second thought, I said, "Sure, fire away!"

Neil was a tremendous kisser. He kissed me for so long that, for a moment, I lost track of time. He was very thorough and made sure that you were enjoying every moment. Oh boy, I enjoyed that long kiss. Then, he sat down on this big chair ottoman. He was kind of sprawled out, almost hanging on the chair. I, on the other hand, was feeling aggressive.

After a while, I asked him, "Would you like a blowjob?" Now, that's a question you usually would never get a "no" answer to.

As expected, he replied, "Sure, please go right ahead."

So, I got between his legs to face him and proceeded to give him my finest blowjob, number one quality. It didn't take long for him to cum right there and then. By the time he came, he was sprawled out on this chair ottoman thing looking extremely sexy. I decided it was the perfect time to fuck him.

Let me remind you that Neil was from the younger generation that gladly used a condom. Trust me, when I say this, I found it extremely difficult to get older guys to acquiesce to using condoms. When I got on top of him, he immediately asked, "Do you have condoms?"

I replied instantly, "Sure, let me get one from my room. Stay right there!"

After that, I went to my bedroom, got him a condom, and put it on. We fucked, and it was absolutely remarkable. He was really good. Neil had a lot of stamina, and he was hard the entire time we were fucking. At the same time, he had the perfect size cock, just the way I liked it.

Now that I look back, he had his hands all over me when he came. By this point, I had already come a couple of times at least. In other words, it was a lovely evening—one that I would easily rank as one of the best encounters of my life.

Luckily, this was not a one-time thing. After that night, I played tennis with Neil some more, and it would usually follow a similar pattern. After our tennis session, we would end up back at my place for much wonderful fucking. It is important to note that every time we fucked, Neil brought something new to the table, so sex never became stale; Neil would go out of his way to pleasure me.

One day, Neil just showed up in the middle of the afternoon, hopped over my fence, and asked me, "Can I go swimming?"

I replied, "Sure, I don't have a problem with that one bit."

Then, before long, he took off all his clothes, along with his tennis whites. He was totally ripped, with the sunlight shining on each one of his abs. It was really something; Neil seemed almost godlike. In the next second, he got in the pool and turned around and around. In the pool, he was almost facing me with full frontal nudity. I loved it, and I couldn't really keep my eyes away from his wonderful cock.

He then said, "I'm getting cold. Can I have a towel?"

I responded gleefully, "Sure!"

Immediately, I went to the bathroom, got him a huge beach towel, and wrapped him up in it. Neil claimed that he was still cold. As a result, I took him upstairs to my room and put him into bed. After that, I covered him up with quilts.

By the time he had warmed up a little bit, we had proceeded to fuck some more. He was not in any way reticent about going down on me, which I loved. I returned the favor and then some. All in all, our tryst was rather interesting. Even though I did not really end up pursuing tennis in the long run, I'll always remember the time I had with Neil fondly.

I could never forget those nights back at my house in which we fucked our brains out. The very nights that involved Neil playing with my tits, sucking on me, and generally being a very clever young man. Oh man, what fun we had together. To be honest, it's a shame it had to end. I would've loved to fuck him some more. I'm pretty sure he'd want the same. I wish him all the best and hope that he reads this book and learns just how good he was.

Chapter 17:

High School Antics

This is a rather cautionary tale. You can even call it just a small vignette of sex. I'm saying this because this *relationship* didn't last that long, nor was it one of the more ideal flings I had over the course of my life. Let's just say he was not your typical run-of-the-mill guy. Don't worry! As always, I will reveal all the details so that you, too, can know what I'm talking about. So, let's get cracking.

During my high school years, I started going out with this guy who was absolutely gorgeous. He was six foot five, had this perfect body, and was extremely attractive. This guy was an ex-Green Beret. As a result, he was very well cut. This added to his already impressive personality. He was very tough, and from the get-go, you could tell that he wouldn't tolerate anyone's bullshit. In other words, he was totally my kind of guy. And as I'd recall, I was attracted to him instantly.

He was one of my riding instructor's college buddies. They had known each other for a long time, and he had even seen a lot of action in Vietnam War. Now that I look back, I met him during one of the horse shows. He was very charming, the kind of guy I'm usually attracted to. So, as you would've guessed, I started lusting for him.

Eventually, we began liking each other, and I started going out with him. He'd pick me up and take me down to his trashy apartment. Oh boy, was his apartment fucked up! He had dirty sheets and dishes that hadn't been cleaned—a real mess. But it didn't matter because we were doing something far more important, fucking our brains out.

We'd fuck as hard as we could, and there was no holding back. We were able to keep up with each other, and it was amazing. He was really good in bed. He knew how to pleasure a woman the right way. But if I'm being honest, every time we fucked, I was scared of him. Why? Because, quite frankly, he was not right in the head. Nowadays, we would say he probably had PTSD. He had these weird mood swings, and he would wake up in the middle of the night shouting and screaming. He had these horrible nightmares and was pretty unstable. Yet still, he was great in bed, and in all honesty, I loved fucking him.

I do remember one particular incident which really disgusted me beyond imagination—the day before I was supposed to take the SATs. I was with him the night before. Instead of concentrating on the SATs, we fucked, and he told me to lick his balls. The very concept of this *act* had not yet registered for me. I couldn't believe that this was actually part of oral sex.

In fact, I didn't even think that he was going to ask me this of me. Yet, he did, and I regretfully complied. As expected, it was horrible. I was awfully close to his ass, way more than I'd ever allowed under normal circumstances. It was really gross, and it freaked me out completely. However, I went along with it because I was afraid of his reaction.

The next day, I came up with a plan to end our tryst once and for all. This plan was terribly wrong, and I can see how guys can get accused of raping someone when they didn't. It is very easy, especially if the circumstances support the girl's claim. A guy could be in deep trouble. Anyway, coming back, I was very hungover for the SATs. I told my friends that he had forced me to have sex with him.

I did this because some of my friends would give me a hard time about my sexuality. They believed that I wasn't telling the truth and I was some kind of lesbian. Because they had not seen me with a guy from school. It was very childish and annoying, and I thought me telling the story would solve two of my problems. Now that I look back, lots of my friends were screwing around but not talking about it.

On the contrary, I was very open about what I was up to. If things had gone wrong and the word had spread to everyone in school, he could have been charged with sexual assault. It would've happened all because of me lying about that night. But thankfully, only a select few of my friends knew, and they kept everything hush-hush. However, word had reached the guy, and he simply stopped seeing me. He was well aware of the consequences, so he thought it was best to call it quits right there and then. I moved on because, frankly, I had to concentrate on much more important things.

Before we go any further, I would like to point out that there were plenty of other things than sex in my life. In fact, in all honesty, I had a lot on my table. Among them were the various things I got away with in high school due to my academic achievements. As I'd recall, I was a real politician. Why you ask? Because I practically charmed as many of my teachers and administrators as I could. This, in turn, allowed me to get away with murder, so to speak. Boy, what fun I had! It was pretty exhilarating.

At the same time, I had a good friend who used to love to get into misadventures with me. From seventh grade on, I would go to school on St. Patrick's Day with green carnations, dressed in a kilt, and would go from all my classrooms to the homerooms first thing in the morning. I'd be wearing bright lime green stockings with my kilt, give my teachers a carnation, and say, "Top of the morning to you, now."

My friend and I then shifted our focus toward painting bright green paint down the middle of the road, which circled around the three sides of our very large high school. One year, it snowed, and we still put the paint down. It wasn't too hard to figure out who had done this, but I never got in any trouble for it. I was that discreet and charming, the school's delight. No one could've ever imagined that I'd do something like this. I was the perfect criminal, so to speak.

Other than this, we did things like move all the desks—well, truth be told, I organized this. In Spanish class, we had this Cuban Spanish teacher. She had the room set up backward. Whenever the office had to talk to her, she had to walk toward the back of the room to the door that left the classroom. She had a giant purse and these brocade suits, which I think she made by herself. There was no way these suits were being sold in the market. They were pretty bad, and teasing her became all the more enjoyable. To be honest, both Janet and I were terrible to her.

One day, we locked her out of the classroom. We did this by taking all of the desks and chairs and putting them on the flat roof of the gymnasium, which was outside the Spanish classroom. She couldn't get in and screamed in Spanish the entire time. It was hilarious. By the time the janitor came and opened the door, everyone sat in their seats and didn't say a word. Also, we would cheat terribly on her tests. We'd go up there with the answers written on our hands or on the next page. She never had a clue what was going on. We passed with flying colors while having the time of our lives.

Another outrageous thing we did was on the day we were graduating—well, that was quite a day in itself. I smoked pot for the very first time, which I liked quite a bit. I borrowed Dona's little brother's banana seat bicycle. You know, one of those little bicycles with the big handlebars and the banana seat. I then wore a bikini with my riding chaps and rode the bicycle all over high school. Our high school was connected with ramps as it had been built over many years. In other words, it was the perfect environment for riding a bicycle.

That morning, Janet and I had taken what I can only imagine was something along the line of Agent Orange, which my mother used to kill weeds. You'd never be able to sell it in the modern day or for decades previously. As I mentioned, the school was huge. In fact, there was a large half-circle driveway that went in front of the school, filled with grass.

We took a watering can with this Agent Orange stuff and drew; I would guess we drew about 50 feet high, a 70.

We did this because I graduated in 1970. The circle and the zero had a peace sign in the middle. Frankly, we were all against the Vietnam War. We were deeply concerned about our brothers and our friends and wondered if they would ever get drafted. So, naturally, we felt that the best course of action was to end the war immediately.

It has been more than ten years, and the grass still would not grow in that 70. That 70 stood on the front lawn all through college for me, a symbol of what I could get away with. It was pretty flattering. We would get into all sorts of other escapades. In most cases, I was always looking to get away with a stiffy and was normally up to many high jinks. It was a truckload of fun, and I enjoyed every day of high school. Regrettably, it was coming to an end.

The following year was my senior year in high school. And as you can see, I was in the habit of getting into all sorts of trouble at school but not getting caught. I only went to the classes that I liked and found challenging. Some of these classes included Latin, English Literature, Chemistry, and various other difficult subjects like that.

I was once brought in by my algebra teacher for cheating. He made this insinuation because I would do eight steps of algebra in my head. He was pretty sure that I was cheating. He couldn't possibly believe that a student would solve the equation mentally. He was under this false assumption for a long time until I did it in front of him. I showed him that I could skip 8 or 10 steps and then come up with a number to kind of mark my place in my thought processes. He was astonished, and it was a very proud moment for me. Even though I had somewhat of an idea regarding my intelligence, seeing the look of amazement on my teacher's face sold the deal for me. I knew that I could achieve and do many great things in life.

Then, before long, we had the graduation ceremony in the large auditorium. I, on my mortar board, took white tape—our colors were navy blue—and taped a circle with the peace sign with the seven before it. I made the digits 70. I was so tall that no one—none of the teachers or anyone picked up on this. However, I'm sure everyone in the audience could see it, certainly from the balcony section of the school. It was another sublime moment for me, and the entire ceremony is still engraved in my mind. This marked the end of an era for me, and I went on to even greener pastures.

Chapter 18:

Off to College

After graduating from high school, I had to face yet another great challenge in my life. This challenge was none other than doing very well on the SATs. Even though I had graduated from high school with good grades, it still didn't guarantee my admission into a prestigious college.

For that, I needed to pass the SATs, and that too with flying colors. Otherwise, I wouldn't be able to get into any decent college. So, naturally, I was very stressed out and couldn't wait for my results. I had my fair share of escapades in high school, and I didn't want them to adversely affect my academic future. All I could do now was hope for the best, and the wait was killing me.

Thankfully, the gods were kind to me. I got twin 800s on the SATs. This meant that I could basically pick any college I wanted to go to. I was so happy that as soon as I opened the mail, I hugged my mother as hard as I could. I told her my results gleefully. She congratulated me and told me to start applying for colleges. I followed her instruction, and Justine Jane shepherded me through this whole process.

Let me point out that in this regard, my parents were of no help. They didn't seem to have a clue regarding what I had to do to get into college. So, the only person I could turn to at this crucial moment was Justine. As expected, she helped me through and through. I ended up applying to some of the colleges she applied to. We ended up going to the same college. It's generally not recommended that two high school best friends also then go off to college together. But in our case, we were inseparable. And now, our new journey was about to begin.

The time had come for me to go to college. As I mentioned, Justine and I had both picked the same college to go to and even convinced the dean that we could be roommates. It was only the second year the college had allowed girls in.

There was a book that was put out with the girls' pictures in it. I think it probably had the guys' pictures too. So, I put in one of my modeling pictures. All the while,

Justine, who was so cute, put in just some regular pictures. This picture was from her time as a cheerleader.

Before long, we had all the boys coming by to check us out. Why, you ask? Was it because we were exceptionally pretty girls? Well, even if I wanted this to be true, that wasn't the case. In reality, the other girls were shy valedictorians of their Pennsylvania high school or something. In other words, they were very nerdy girls that simply didn't want to work on themselves or attract boys. On the other hand, Justine and I were experienced young women willing to go to town, so to speak. And the boys realized this just by looking at our pictures in the book.

Eventually, we arrived with everything we had in a horse trailer. When we reached our dorm, we unpacked and then convinced the dean we had to paint our room. We did this because it was such a horrible institutionalized green color. We couldn't possibly live there. She let us change the colors.

You can even say that by going to college, I became a great interior designer. I couldn't tolerate the color of the room and knew it had to change. Ultimately, with grace, we managed to convince the dean that not only should we be roommates together but that we were allowed to paint the room white.

I had an old American flag that probably had 40 stars on it or something. We hung that across our window like a curtain. The security people came and said we couldn't have that flag hanging in our window. They claimed that we were disrespecting the flag.

Let me remind you that this was the era of the Cold War and the Vietnam War was ongoing. And naturally, we were against the war, and the flag was our form of protest. However, we were so good at convincing people of things that Justine and I convinced security that we did this to honor the flag. We said something along the lines of, "Don't worry, we put the flag up there because we are so proud of our nation! We're not disrespecting anything or anyone. This is our nation's pride."

Agreeing with what we had to say, security left, and the flag hung there until I left the dorm. We had these two big posters. One was *Butch Cassidy And The Sundance Kid.* The other was of Peter Fonda on his chopped motorcycle in

Easy Rider, which had come out the previous year. At the same time, we also had a poster of Kyle Singer, who will have his own chapter in this book.

We were the second co-ed class at Franklin and Marshall, one of the top pre-veterinarian pre-med schools in the country. Basically, if you passed there with decent grades, you could get into any medical or veterinary school. Regretfully, during this time, there were still people that discouraged me from being a vet. However, I didn't listen and pursued my studies enthusiastically.

I had, of course, been busy acquiring some new lovers at college. There was a rather hysterical fraternity. There was this fraternity house, but it was like *Animal House.* All the Greek letters were written upside down. It was pretty clear that they'd been banned from college.

The head of this group of crazy guys was called "Captain America." As soon as we met, we took a shine to each other. He would wear capes and had this thick curly black hair. He was very attractive and also extremely sexual. We'd go out often and, of course, fucked each other's brains out. There was a great river outside Lancaster. We'd all go there and go skinny dipping. We had lots of fun.

I had one other lover while I was there. He was cute. He rode a motorcycle, and I, for one, hated riding motorcycles. I didn't find them appealing one bit and would never ride one. I did have a moped later on in college, which is pretty much a ridiculous motorcycle. The reason being a moped is so underpowered. However, I had no problem riding the guy every chance we had. It was really fun, and he was pretty experienced in riding women and motorcycles.

I had mainly taken the sciences. Although I also had an English Literature course. Justine had her own stuff that she was doing. We didn't share any classes, but Justine was always with a boyfriend. In fact, she had a boyfriend who was at Cornell. He was absolutely crazy for her. He couldn't stomach the fact that Justine was down in Lancaster, Pennsylvania, wanting to break up with him and date other people.

Two or three times, he drove from Cornell to Pennsylvania in record time and got stopped by the police. Then, he started throwing rocks at our window. Justine, again, explained to him—I think she'd only talked to him on the phone. We didn't have cell phones back then. All we had were regular landlines. So, the only way Justine could contact him was through the telephone. We had a payphone on our floor. She called and convinced Arthur Bolt that he had to leave and not come back. It was probably a very emotional call. But it appeared as if Arthur finally accepted it on some level. Arthur left, and that was the end of their relationship. It didn't take long for Justine to hook up with one of the football players.

In most cases, both Justine and the football player would come to our room at night and fuck. This wasn't fun for me because I could hear them fucking. Our beds were right next to each other. He and Justine would fuck in bed while I was in the room, which was not very considerate. I have sometimes been accused of similar things, but I don't remember going that far. It was very uncomfortable.

At any rate, Justine always had a boyfriend. From the time I became her best friend in fifth grade all the way to college, there was always a guy in her life. She was very perky, a cheerleader, prom queen, smart, and charming. So, as you'd expect, she was used to always having the best boyfriend in school. She used her charm in the right way and was subsequently rewarded. I really liked that about her. In any case, I loved her and still wish her all the best. Everything was going well in college. I had adjusted quite well, but all of a sudden, I had to deal with an emergency. This emergency was my dad's health.

My dad was dying. He was only 47. I knew he was dying. On the other hand, my mother didn't even believe this was possible because we all called him "The Giant." That was his nickname, The Giant. My mother, who adored him and had a great marriage overall, couldn't accept how sick he was. She was in denial and couldn't face up to this reality. I tried convincing her, but it was to no avail.

At the same time, I was faced with a conundrum. I loved the college, but I knew my dad was dying. I had to take care of him. So, I decided to move home to spend as much time with him as I could. It turned out that my father had testicular cancer, which had metastasized. He wasn't going to recover. All we could do was wait and take care of him as much as we could.

Unfortunately, he died at 47, which was a huge blow to my family—one that my mother didn't recover from for a long time. Luckily, I had the privilege of spending a couple of good years with him. I also helped take care of him, and for that, I'm eternally grateful. My brother was in the submarine service. My good friend Shay's father, who owned the largest chemical company in New Jersey, somehow contacted Rodino.

Rodino was the chairman of the Nixon Impeachment Committee overseeing the whole Watergate thing. Shay's father convinced Rodino to somehow airlift my brother off a submarine somewhere in the world and bring him back home to New Jersey. He did this so my brother could be there for my father's funeral. This was a huge favor, and my brother didn't appreciate what he had done for him. In fact, in all honesty, I didn't even realize this until later when I pieced everything together. Shay turned out to be a great friend, and I'll always hold her in the highest regard.

After that, I decided to move home from Franklin to Marshall permanently. There was a great school in New York that did not have undergraduate degrees called the

New School for Social Research. This school was founded for the refugees fleeing Hitler and was a social sciences school. They only did Master's degrees and PhD programs.

Fortunately, after a while, they were about to start a BA program or undergraduate degree program with different programs from all over the New York area. This program involved various universities and people who wrote for *The Economist* about the UN. In other words, they provided a quality education.

My political science professor wrote for *The Economist*. He would bring ambassadors in from the UN. One week, he would bring the Egyptian Ambassador to class, and the next week, the Israeli Ambassador. They would tell us their side of the story. It was pretty enlightening. The whole semester was like that, and I got to learn a lot. I also had an incredible philosophy professor. These were the senior courses.

The school also specialized (even to this day) in large, popular courses in auditoriums regarding film, music, or whatever. We used to jokingly call these "Underwater Volkswagen Beetle Repair Courses." These courses didn't have any credit. In fact, they were really a completely different part of the school.

When I enrolled in the school, my mom let me have her car most of the time to go to New York. As a result, I didn't have to take the bus. Also, since my brother was away in the submarine service, I'd get to use his cargo van. Now that I look back, it was more like his drug mobile. Why do I say that? Well, the short answer is that my brother was a big druggie, drug dealer, and eventually, drug importer. It was a great source of disappointment for me. But what could I do? In the end, every one of us lives different lives. I just hoped he'd done something productive in his life. But alas, that wasn't meant to be.

I had a couple of great friends at that school. There was this one guy who brought me to McSorely's Ale House. During this time, they were not allowing women to drink. So, taking me, there was a huge deal. Because of this guy, the people at McSorely's had to allow women there. When a woman would come in there, they'd ring a big bell. It was pretty weird. Yet still, my friend would take me there regularly.

As you would've guessed, he obviously wanted to be my lover. He definitely had a huge crush on me and was really nice and smart. He would've been a great boyfriend. However, unfortunately, I was not really good at picking great boyfriends. I had a knack for picking lovers but not long-term boyfriends. This was just something about me. And because of my habit, nothing ever happened between us.

I've always reflected on this and wondered why I didn't like this guy. To be honest, I should've gone out with that guy and not just been messing around or whatever. I was fairly fond of this new style, but I guess it wasn't meant to be. I am a big believer that if something is meant to happen, it will happen. So, me not hooking up with that guy was probably for the best. After all, I did live a colorful life, so in the long haul, everything worked out. And knowing this, I couldn't be happier.

Chapter 19:

Michelle Mustain

Even though I was focusing on my studies and aiming for good grades, I didn't lose sight of my other passion, horse riding. In fact, all throughout college, I went to various horse shows.

For me, horse riding was something I couldn't live without. It was irreplaceable in my view. And in all honesty, I wasn't about to let college or any other thing deter me from my passion. That's why I kept on attending as many horse shows as I could. There was no stopping me, and I enjoyed every second I got to spend with the horses. It was one of these horse shows in which I met a woman I really admired.

I got a job grooming for a local at one of the bigger horse shows. Now, this person was a well-known crazy in my town. He lived very near to where my barn was. At the same time, he was about to show up with one of the up-and-coming stars of the horse show world, Richard Harris.

Let me also point out that Richard had been on the Olympic team in Tokyo in '64. Richard is the only Olympic rider to represent the US in eventing, show jumping, and dressage. He was gorgeous. And Richard was just starting to do the open jumpers. Open jumpers are none other than the big fences where you have to go as high and as fast as you can.

During this time, I had a deal with a guy in New Vernon. I called him Jolly Cholly or the Pillsbury Dough Boy. He was a customer of Richard. Richard was going to be riding his horses, and he was supposed to get me a Holiday Inn room.

I remember being paid a certain amount. I received instructions that I would only be taking care of Jolly Cholly's four horses. For that, obviously, I had to head over to his farm. I thought, *Fine, I'll take care of the horses. I'm sure they are beautiful and well-behaved. This will be a walk in the park.*

I didn't have any issues with my new job. But by the time I reached his farm, it got really weird. I'm sure you're wondering why I'm saying this. Well, the simple reason is that when I told Jolly that I was about to come over, he claimed that he lived alone. However, the moment I reached his farm, I saw his mother peeking out of the third-story window. It was literally like a scene from *Psycho*.

With some hesitation, I began by spending my first couple of hours grooming the horses. The horses were fine but spending time at his barn was pretty challenging. I kept on thinking about his mother and started looking here and there to make sure I wasn't being attacked. It was very tense, but thankfully, I got through it. I figured he probably forgot to inform me about his mother and continued grooming his horses.

After a while, we went to Pennsylvania to Doylestown to this big horse show. Charlie (Jolly) did not attend the show and failed to get me a room. At the same time, he reneged on how much he was going to pay me. This was a very underhanded move from him, and I kind of expected it. He was a creepy man, and you could expect anything from him. Seeing no other choice, I gave the four horses to Richard and his girlfriend, Michelle Mustain (Michelle), along with all of Charlie's good show bridles. I did this to receive payment for taking the horses. In my mind, it was a fair deal for all the hard work I'd put in.

After this deal, I became very good friends with Michelle rather quickly. There were a bunch of reasons for this. But among them, I believe the main reason was that Michelle was just a very easy-going person. You could relate to her in every way, and you could talk to her about anything. In other words, Michelle had a lot of qualities, and I immediately befriended her.

Strangely enough, Michelle was from Canada, just south of where I spent my summer vacations. When I heard this, I remember thinking, *What a strange coincidence? It is almost as if we are fated to meet. Boy, this is exciting!*

At the same time, Michelle was an extremely stylish and great beauty. She was a little older than I was, so she took me under her wing. She would teach me everything there was to know about horses. It was pretty obvious that she had done a lot of horse riding in her life. She was a wonderful teacher, and we had lots of fun riding together. Eventually, I ended up going back with Michelle and Richard back to their farm in New Hope, which was a tremendous experience in itself.

With the passage of time, Michelle and I had become so close that there was practically nothing happening in our life that we didn't share with one another. We had become best pals and would guide each other as much as we could. When James left me behind and went to France with Michelle and Richard, she brought me back a bottle of Joy Perfume.

This was the same perfume Michelle used on a regular basis, and I absolutely loved it. We palled around together. One day, she came to me with some information that I already had. This new *insight* was that Richard was cheating on her. She came to me and said, "I know he's cheating on me. I just know it. Don't you dare try to convince me otherwise."

Unfortunately, as fate would have it, Richard was actually having an affair with one of my other best friends. This best friend was none other than Rosemary, someone I'd known for quite some time. I have a rather hysterical story about Rosemary, Shelly, and I getting into trouble, which I will disclose in another chapter.

Michelle also stated, "I don't know what to do. What should I do? I love Richard. How could he do this to me? Why did he do this? Oh god, I can't believe it. Please, tell me something."

She further added, "There are only two people in the country that Richard would be pissed if I left him for them. This would be either Frank or Russ. I think I need to hook up with one of them. I have to teach Richard a lesson. He went too far. Now, he will get a taste of his own medicine."

I replied in a serious tone, "Michelle, Frank's great, but he's a country boy. You're very sophisticated; he's not. Yes, he's at this time the greatest rider in America, but that doesn't mean shit. You're way better than he'll ever be. Don't sell yourself short. So, your only real choice is Russ."

I told her that Russ was perfect for her. I told her he was gorgeous, an incredible rider, and an impeccable course designer. In fact, Russ was pretty young as well. This was mainly because he was younger than I was. And I, on the other hand, was younger than Michelle. So, in other words, it was a perfect match for Michelle, and she agreed. I don't know how the breakup actually happened, but she ended up leaving Richard and hooking up with Russ.

As it turned out, Michelle would go on to marry Russ and even have a child with him. I think, at least, she had one kid with Russ. And, from what I've heard, they've been a great couple. They spend all winter in Florida at the big Palm Beach horse show.

Now that I look back, Michelle was always the most stylish person that you'd see at the horse show. She just had a way of putting clothes together and scarves. At the same time, she had this beautiful hair. If you'd ask me, Michelle deserved to have everything work in her favor. Why? Because she was a great person.

Richard was being a total shit to her, and she deserved all the best in the world. Though, it really put me in an awkward position because, quite frankly, I wanted to be with Russ. However, she was one of my best friends, and she had approached him first. And now, after all these years, I'm very happy with the life she's carved out for herself.

Chapter 20:

Lust

Oddly enough, when I was writing this chapter, I had just finished watching the show *Billions* on TV. In it, Axe, the main character, is making love for the first time to a new woman. This scene reminded me so much of Terry Cooper. Because, to be honest, Axe and Terry look very much alike; both have the same dark red hair, the swagger, along with that "not really caring what the fuck anybody else thinks" attitude—a trait that I love dearly.

It was one of the main reasons why I fell for Terry in the first place. His "devil may care" attitude is something we both have in common. I also cared less about what other people thought of me. For me, living life as I see fit matters more than anything else. And seeing this quality, I fell head over heels for Terry and cherish the time we spent together even to this day.

Anyway, coming back to the show, Axe was up on his elbows, kissing her neck and pushing his cock into her hard and slow. He kept on pushing his cock in for quite a while until the girl started making the sounds of pleasure. It was so satisfying to watch and reminded me of the lovemaking I had with Terry, especially when he'd have his hair hanging down in my face. The same kind of lovemaking in which Terry would make it a point to touch and kiss me all over the body. Just like the woman in the show, I, too, would be releasing sounds of pleasure with my lungs off with every stroke. Boy, that was amazing!

In fact, Terry would be pushing his cock masterfully and as deep as he could into me. As you'd imagine, I absolutely loved it. I couldn't control my emotions and would just pant like there was no tomorrow. Much like the scene, Terry would hold me up by the shoulders and go on to run his hands up and down my sides and over my breasts. In all honesty, the moment his hands touched my breast, I felt wet and almost came that instant. It was exhilarating, to say the least, and Terry would make sure that I was comfortable before he went any further. What a perfect gentleman!

On occasion, Terry would kiss me, and when he did, he always kissed my neck, which I loved. He did this simply because he knew I loved it. In other words, Terry was a lover that not only knew what he was doing but what his partner expected of him. Trust me when I say that this is very rare. Normally, in lovemaking, lovers only care about themselves and not their better half. That's why relationships end up falling apart so easily. They don't do what's necessary for lovemaking, and the chemistry simply fades out with time.

This brings me to a rather important question that many people don't have an answer to, "What is good lovemaking?" If you'd ask me, I think it's, first of all, figuring out what your partner wants, what they like, and what they don't like, and then giving it to them. It's rather simple, provided you put your partner's needs above your own.

Doing something which your partner likes might not be that off-putting. I can say from experience that there were many positions of lovemaking that I didn't like that much before but absolutely loved after doing them. A classic example of this is giving blowjobs. At first, I didn't even know how to give blowjobs, but when I learned to give a perfect blowjob, I started loving the act. So, try to give your partner the benefit of the doubt and always be open-minded. You never know what you may end up liking in the long haul.

For me, I definitely preferred having hands all over my body. You know that wonderful feeling you get when your lover starts working their way down from your neck to your lips to sucking on your breasts, licking them, and kissing them. Not long after that, they'd just keep moving down and start licking around your belly button. Then, they'd start working their way from your belly button down to your pussy, spreading your legs, licking, and sucking on your labia and your clit. Oh, I especially liked it when they wouldn't stop there. Instead, they would start kissing your legs and begin the process all over again.

In my experience, that is a magnificent feeling, truly irreplaceable. Why you ask? Well, the simple answer is that, during the process, you can see yourself being loved for real and not only in your imagination. For me, this really seals the deal. Also, I really loved it when my lover would turn me over on my stomach, rub my back, kiss my back, go on to kiss the back of my neck, and then proceed to kiss me all over my body.

In my opinion, that's wonderful, masterful lovemaking. This is especially the case when your lover has you on your stomach, and they proceed to slide their cock into your pussy to again continue fucking you and make you cry out their name.

Now, correct me if I'm wrong, but you're absolutely loving it at this point and can't wait to call out their names. Am I right? Of course, I am because I've had that kind of lovemaking. Truth be told, I want that again in my life. I want Terry again and all my wonderful lovers of the past so that I can relive those moments over and over again. Perhaps, I'll have this opportunity in the future. And if that ever happens, don't worry; you'll definitely know.

For those of you who still don't understand what wonderful lovemaking is, I want to elaborate further on the experiences I had. If I'm being honest, I loved having my fingers sucked, my palms licked, and my lovers swirling around their tongues up the inside of my arm. At the same time, I loved it when they worked their way down from my neck and when they were partially down my stomach. At this crucial moment of intense pleasure, I grab hold of my lover's cock and start sucking it, sucking it really well.

Why? Because I want to inspire him to give me the best head he can, nibble on my thighs, and lick my pussy. I think there's a theme here regarding things that I like, and I even like my toes sucked on. Let me point out that I keep my feet very clean, so there's nothing gross or weird about it. I also look forward to the wonderful feeling of watching your lover over you and pushing inside. Then, I love watching them collapse on top of me, grabbing me around the back and the waist and turning me over, and pulling me down toward him.

As I've mentioned repeatedly throughout this book, I LOVE to be on top. I love that feeling of absolute control in which you can bring yourself to cum, maybe even multiple times if you're lucky. At the same time, you get to laugh, play, and have him pull you up and fuck your pussy from behind.

These are all wonderful things that every girl deserves to experience many times in their life. Because these moments are very erotic and make you cum right there and then, that's also the moment when your lover asks if you've cum enough, and you passionately say, "Yes."

Then, they proceed to fuck you even more intensely. Because by this point, they know you are completely satiated and that they can now take you the way they want. Perhaps this will explain what I mean by "masterful, wonderful lovemaking."

In my view, this is the right of every person, whether they are a man or a woman. Instead of moralizing and suppressing ourselves, we need to love as hard and as masterfully as we can. Only then can we experience real happiness and intimacy on a far greater level.

Chapter 21:

Variety

At this point, I don't know how many more lovers I should discuss. Because from what I've shared in previous chapters, you can see that I've had my fair share of experiences. In fact, I can easily say that my trysts have been extremely interesting. Apart from a few exceptions, I always had great sexual encounters. Every lover I've had brought something new to the table, so to speak. At the same time, most of them went out of their way to make sure I was satisfied on all fronts.

Yes, there had been a few oddballs and awkward moments here and there. But generally, almost all of my lovers had brought their A-game in bed, which I enjoyed quite a lot. Maybe I'll share a few more experiences to help you understand what I'm talking about. In the end, I don't want to bore you.

No, not at all. I want you to read this book and feel as entertained as humanly possible. I don't want you to think of my book as a run-of-the-mill autobiography filled with boring encounters and reminiscences. On the contrary, I want you to read this book and feel inspired. I want you to realize that you, too, can live a life according to your own terms. Just like me, you can make your own decisions and enjoy life to the fullest.

If there's anything I'd like you to take away from this book, it's this: live life intensely and without any regrets. If you can embrace this principle, I'll know that I achieved something worthwhile in my life. Because this is my life's motto, and through it, I've been able to live a life that only people can dream of. And thankfully, I've no regrets whatsoever. Why should I regret being happy? Why should I have any qualms about having sex? I'll live my life as I see fit. And you should do the same. That's the only way you can be truly happy. So, if you've not adopted this principle in your life, do it now and live at your full potential. Try to enjoy life as intensely as you can, and I can assure you that you will not be disappointed. Everything you experience will be worth it, and you will explore the real richness of existence. Trust me; I speak from experience, LOTS of experience.

In any case, coming back to the topic at hand, I realized after going over this list that it's all over the place as far as the type of lovers I have cultivated over the years. I have mentioned lovers that are rich, poor, horse people, townspeople, teachers, and students. But, in all honesty, they're a really great group. The ones I've mentioned are undoubtedly the cream of the crop. Because, through them, I learned a great deal about myself and the act of sex which I hold dear. In other words, I owe it all to them, and that's why they became a part of this book.

Now, don't get me wrong, I can easily go on; I have plenty more candidates that I can add in later chapters. However, these lovers are just not as stellar as the ones I've mentioned before for whatever reason. That's why I'm rethinking whether I should share these exploits or not. I think I might just share a couple of juicy stories. You guys deserve that.

Again, it still eludes me how I could really describe why I would be attracted to someone and why it would or would not work out. To be honest, I don't have a definitive answer for this. Relationships are complicated. You may never know what you're doing wrong until it's too late. At the same time, certain relationships run their natural course. And frankly, there's no way to save them, no matter how hard you try.

That's why, in this book, I made it a point not to focus on why relationships don't work out sometimes. I know for a fact that the relationship not working out could be my fault as well, not just the guy's. I have the integrity to admit that I might be wrong and partly to blame. There are always two sides to a situation. And, in all honesty, I'm not the kind of woman to always blame the guys.

In many cases, you're just not a match for unknown reasons. In other words, there's nothing you can do, and before long, both of you are living different lives, which is fine if you ask me. What is meant to work WILL work out in the end. So, don't beat yourself up about it. Just move on and look forward to what the universe has in store for you.

In my case, I love to fuck. I love it to a fault. In my opinion, there's no real substitute for sex and physical intimacy. I need it in a relationship; otherwise, it won't work out at all. However, let me point out that I don't like giving handjobs. I never have, and I never will because, quite frankly, I missed that stage. There were no handjobs in my sex life. I experimented with all kinds of positions and sexual acts but never handjobs.

Although this doesn't necessarily mean that I minded a man that was good with his hands, no, not at all; in fact, I even preferred it. I just didn't feel like I was any good with my hands. I was very good at other positions, and I loved to please a man as much as I could. However, I was not that easy or even comfortable with giving handjobs.

Instead, I'd rather scratch the guy's back, rub their back or grab their butt or do something of the sort. At the same time, I do love to kiss. For me, kissing is a magnificent art that you can only master through constant practice. In my view, a good kisser is a passionate creature. In my experience, normally, if the guy likes to kiss, they WILL kiss you everywhere. In such scenarios, I knew I was in for a good time. These men are well aware that they've perfected kissing into an art form. As a result, they want to show it off, and thank God for that.

In the end, it's all a mixed bag if you ask me. There is a hockey player, a society boy, and other members of a funny group. If they're in this beginning group here, they are definitely amongst my favorites. Because they knew how to pleasure a woman the right way, and the memories I have with them are still engraved in my mind. I just hope they never change and continue to pleasure other women because they, too, deserve it!

Chapter 22:

The Pearsons

One of my three best friends growing up was Shay Pearson (Shay). Shay, our friend Justine Jane (Justine), and I were a sort of trio. We were birds of a feather and totally inseparable. All three of us being young, good-looking, and popular, we naturally found each other to be better company than pretty much anyone else. None of us was threatened by the others, so we didn't have to deal with the little rivalries and jealousies that a lot of teenage girls encounter. That was probably why we ended up having so many of our formative experiences around the same time, exploring and experimenting together and sharing our adventures.

One difference with Shay was that she, unlike me and Justine, had a brother like Jason.

Jason was Shay's middle brother. He was quite possibly the coolest guy in the neighborhood. He had a gorgeous Stingray convertible Corvette, and he'd drive

Justine to school in it even though she lived just a block away. That thing would slice through the air between their house and the school building like a knife through hot butter, and it had a similar effect on all of us who stood there watching, waiting for the gravel to crunch. Everyone was jealous because it was such a beautiful car, and Justine got to ride in it every day!

As a young girl, I had a mad, mad crush on Keith Pearson, who was in college at the time. Jason, on the other hand, was Justine's boyfriend. I was young, and the whole world lay before me, and everything was full of possibilities.

In those days, I used to spend a lot of time at the Pearsons' house. I loved being at their place. Truth be told, they spoiled me rotten. I was like another member of the family, only I had it better because I wasn't actually their kid, so I could come and go as I pleased and never had any conflict with them the way that kids always do with their own parents. It was a home away from home, and I felt fully accepted there. I'll give you an example.

As I mentioned earlier, Shay had another brother named was Keith. When we were a bit older, Keith was about to get married, and Shay and her mother were not happy about the girl Keith was marrying. They didn't think it was going to work out, they didn't like her, and they would go so far as to try to put a stop to it if they could.

They kept encouraging me to try to seduce him, which I almost did the night before his wedding. You could say the timing was inappropriate, but hey: what better way to know if a guy's going to get cold feet than by throwing a little temptation in his way? If he falls, you know one of two things: either he doesn't really want to go through with it, or he's going to be unfaithful even if he does go through with it. And if he *doesn't* fall, you can say bravo and let the church bells ring; no harm, no foul.

Anyway, I didn't get the chance to put the moves on Keith until the eleventh hour, so to speak. It was at the Pearsons' house, of course. To my surprise, he was not unresponsive, and I was enjoying myself, too. The two of us were a little way apart from everybody else, and I asked him how he was feeling about the impending nuptials. I asked if he was nervous. He was.

I won't recount the dialogue word for word, but I'll give you the gist. I told him he had no need to be nervous and that he'd be just fine, only it was such a shame that a handsome guy like him was going off the market so soon, which would be sure to disappoint a lot of women. He said, "Really?" He seemed flattered but also like he thought I might be making fun of him. Which I was, to be fair, but then I started to get into the spirit of the thing.

He told me I was kidding him, and I protested that I was not. On the contrary, I myself was one of the women who would be disappointed to see him snapped up for good and all. I'd always thought he was cute, and I had cherished the secret hope that one day, just maybe, he and I might get the chance to have a little fun of our own.

"No way. You're pulling my leg."

"I'm not. I've always had the biggest crush on you. You can't pretend you didn't know …."

You get the picture; I laid it on pretty thick. What had started out as playful banter became flirting, and before you knew it, all the jokiness had gone out of the conversation, and suddenly, the air between us was a lot warmer. Things were starting to heat up. To be honest, I wasn't *totally* putting him on. I had always liked Keith; he was a wonderful gentleman. I had even always wanted to date him, so there was a lot of truth in what I said. If that hadn't been so, I would never have been so convincing in my "act."

"Why don't we go upstairs?"

"What? You mean us? Here? *Now?*"

"Why not? You're getting married tomorrow. We'll never have this chance again."

"Well …."

He really considered it. It was one of those moments. You know, a crossroads. It was crazy, but it wasn't *that* crazy. It's not like we were strangers. I'd been in and out of their house since I was a little girl.

But then, wouldn't you know it, Keith got ahold of himself.

"No, I can't do this."

Like I said, a real gentleman!

We laughed it off later as being all in good fun, but when he and his wife broke up (turns out Shay and Mrs. Pearson were right), we did date. But that was years later.

Yes, life would have been quite different without the Pearsons.

Chapter 23:

Surgeons

Even though my business was surgical microscopes and other surgical equipment, I never went out with a surgeon. I never wanted anyone to think that the surgeons were buying things from me because I had taken them out or that I was fucking them to make sales or something.

In retrospect, it seems like a missed opportunity. After all, in my line of work, merely in the course of conducting business, I'd come into contact with a veritable revolving door of surgeons, and unlike most people who come into contact with surgeons, I was able to give *them* what *they* needed rather than the reverse. Think about it – most people only ever meet a surgeon when they're about to go under the knife. That's a hell of a power imbalance. But I got to reverse that dynamic. Yes, of course, I could benefit from a famous surgeon's endorsement. But unlike basically everyone else, when *I* had dealings with a surgeon, *he* came to *me*.

And yet I never took advantage of my position, which is more than you can say of most surgeons, I promise you. As a breed of men, they're pretty impressed with themselves. They're the rock stars of the medical world, and they know it. Surgeons have actual groupies. And it has a lot to do with the power they hold in their hands. It gives them a masterful air. Sometimes, it's very attractive. Other times, they look at a person like they've been laid out on a table, and that isn't so hot unless that's your thing, of course.

Well, it wasn't mine. I'm a professional.

I did have two lovers that were surgeons. Just two, and with a fairly long interval between the first and the second, but they had one thing in common: they both had wonderful hands. They could touch you just so and make you cum. Great hands, it seems, are a prerequisite for surgery. I don't know if it's a natural gift or a consequence of training; either way, the skills, at least in my experience, are applicable to a wide range of activities.

I'd go as far as to claim that most surgeons easily outperform the hands-on musicians – your guitarists, your pianists, and so on. Guitar players always have terrible calluses, and all that thick, hard skin actually impedes the sensitivity of their fingertips. That's no good. You've got to be able to regulate the pressure of your touch.

Keyboard players don't have that problem, but they're always trying something fancy when they should be focused on the end goal. A woman's body is not a Steinway any more than an orgasm is a *sonata-allegro*.

Maybe it's not even about a person's hands. Maybe it has to do with bodies, plain and simple. A musician is familiar with his instrument, but a surgeon knows the body, has touched all kinds of bodies, and knows his way around. And then surgery is a very deliberate thing; even exploratory surgery has a well-defined goal. There's no room for showing off – you've got a job to do.

What it all adds up to is that both the surgeons I fucked drove me wild with slow, smooth caresses that led into long, firm, deep strokes, and they ran their thumbs around the edges of my nipples and stroked my sides with the backs of their nails and brushed the hollows above my hips and ran their fingers up the backs of my thighs before parting them and finally touching my pussy, where both of them knew exactly what to do.

In retrospect, I wish I had had more surgeons. I don't know why I was so strict about it – just one of my things.

Chapter 24:

Hellen & Erlich

At one point, I employed an answering service for models. This service was recommended to me by a friend of mine, or to be more specific, a friend of James'. Initially, I was a bit skeptical, but when I met the people doing this service, we hit it off right away. It was just one of those moments where you click instantly with the people you meet, even if they're complete strangers. You know, the kind of people that give off a pleasant vibe wherever they go.

Well, in my case, Hellen and Erlich were perfect examples of this. They both had a certain kind of charm that pulled you toward them. I mean, no matter how hard you tried, you couldn't possibly ignore them. They were that magnetic, and it didn't take long for me to become close to them. Hellen and Erlich were teenage lovers who had grown up in the same part of Connecticut.

They were both from Westport. At this point, they were living in New York in a fancy apartment on Sutton Place. As you can imagine, they had family money, both of them. Not everyone could afford a home at Sutton Place. Hellen and Erlich were clearly loaded and knew how to spend their fortunes.

To give you an idea, they had just imported hashish from South America. Just imagine how much money they'd spent to not only buy the hashish but also bring it to the United States. It was really insane. Obviously, Hellen and Erlich had money to burn, and I was about to become their new best friend.

In their Sutton Place home, I remember that they had this really long, fuzzy animal rug that was under the coffee table. It stuck out like a sore thumb, so to speak. You couldn't possibly be in the room and not notice it. It was that conspicuous and clearly very expensive. Anyway, Hellen and Erlich were always dropping hashish on this thing by mistake.

Every time we smoked hash together, they dropped bits and pieces of it on the rug. Yet, they didn't have a care in the world. And when I pointed this out to them, they'd laugh it off and say something along the lines of, "Don't worry! The maid will come in tomorrow. She'll clean it up. That's no big deal, relax."

The next day, the maid would indeed come in, and she would drop to her knees and handpick the hashish bits from the rug, keeping everything she salvaged for herself. For a long time, I believed Hellen and Erlich were perfect for each other. They had a lot in common, they both had a strong family background, they loved to party, and neither of them had a care in the world. They were almost, in a way, the perfect couple, it seemed. And I was genuinely happy for them.

From the first time we met, Hellen and Erlich took a liking to me. I fit very well into their plan, somehow. In their mind, I'd spruced up their answering service thing. I was their savior of sorts, and we were perfect for each another.

Mainly what we liked to do was that the three of us would go out. During this time, I was so naïve that it never occurred to me that they wanted to make the impression that a threesome was going on involving two gorgeous girls.

Never once did I think that this was a possibility. For me, it was just regular old fun and the occasional high.

But later on, I realized what they wanted to show to other people. After all, Hellen was gorgeous. She was tall, always wore high heels, and was almost my height with heels. At the same time, Erlich was very tall and handsome. He didn't have that typical boyish charm. No, on the contrary, he was a man's man, very masculine.

In most cases, we'd go out to dinner at Maxwell's Plum, which was this extravagant stained-glass restaurant in New York. The restaurant had this particular Austrian white wine that Hellen and Erlich liked, and which cost a fortune; in fact, everything was a fortune with them. They paid for everything, including everything I ate or drank. It was almost surreal, in a way. Boy, did they love to spend their money! At one point, I was starting to think that they might never run out.

We would eat, drink, be merry, and gather the strength to stumble out of there. Then, we'd go back to their place and smoke hash. It was wild, to say the least, and I finally learned what "living the high life" really meant. I would drive home most nights. Lord knows how I would get home, but I somehow managed. Thankfully, I didn't get into any accidents or lose my way back. It seemed as if I had some built-in homing device that allowed me to navigate in my high state.

Hellen, Erlich, and I had a couple of years of great fun, which involved getting into lots of trouble, going to the finest restaurants, and making quite a show of ourselves. It was amazing, and it seemed as if this excitement and happiness would last forever. However, sometime later, Hellen and Erlich got into cocaine. And before I knew it, things started to get weird, VERY WEIRD. All I can say is that things were never quite the same between us after that.

Sometime later, just when I was about to start working, we had a huge snowstorm up in the Connecticut Metro Area. Erlich told me to come over. He claimed that Hellen would be there in a little bit. It snowed, snowed some more, and snowed in more ways than one. Hellen didn't show up.

At this time, Erlich had what I'd guess was probably the first hit of crack cocaine, or maybe it was meth or something. I did it, and I became super sick and paranoid almost instantly. I had always been afraid of being in this situation with him, alone, without Hellen there. Why? Because I knew for a fact that Erlich had fancied me, but I didn't trust him one bit. He tried his best, but I didn't even show the slightest bit of interest. After all, Hellen was my best friend; I couldn't possibly betray her trust even when her man was more than willing.

As I'd expected, the night passed, and Hellen never showed up. In the morning, I somehow drove home through three-foot snow drifts to my mom's house, which luckily was not very far away. On the way there, I was scared beyond belief. It was such a weird feeling. I was so paranoid that somebody was following me.

All I wanted was to reach my mother's doorstep as soon as possible. And thank god; eventually, I made it to my mother's. I was in bed for a week. I don't know what was in that drug, but it was awful. I kept on having nightmares for weeks after that night. It was dreadful, and I kept myself sober for quite some time after that.

Surprisingly enough, this was not a one-time thing. Looking back, I had a prior incident with Hellen and Erlich that involved drug importing. One fateful day, they called me up and said, "Oh, we have a friend who's flying up here. We're going to a party. He could pick you up at Teterboro, which is the private plane airport in northern New Jersey. Would you like to come? C'mon, it'll be fun!"

Hearing this, I replied excitedly, "Sure."

I either got a ride or drove there. Eventually, we got on the plane. Not long after, the plane was airborne. If I'm being honest, the journey was fun. Eventually, we landed in Redding, or as close to Redding, Connecticut, as we could get.

As it turned out, Erlich had close to a ton of cocaine with him. Now that I look back, Hellen and Erlich had probably used me as a mule. By bringing me along, even if Hellen and Erlich were ever forced to stop, they'd have the excuse of picking up this New Jersey girl (me) and then taking off. It was clever on their part but very underhanded. Because, to be honest, I considered them my real friends. So, in a way, I felt hurt.

Anyway, after touchdown, they literally poured a pile of cocaine that was, I believe, close to a foot high. We started snorting it. As usual, I figured if they could snort it, I could snort it, too. And there I was, snorting as much as the boys were. We were getting totally hammered and slightly paranoid. We stayed up all night. The next day, we returned back to New Jersey and resumed our routines as it if had never happened.

This was another weird Hellen and Erlich experience—one that I possibly won't forget my entire life. To be honest, I don't even know what happened between us three. But eventually, we stopped seeing each other. Perhaps Hellen had heard about Erlich and me alone that night in the snowstorm. Maybe I just couldn't deal with their shenanigans anymore. Who knows?

In the end, it was just one of those things. In any case, wherever Hellen and Erlich are, I hope they're together and happy. I wish them all the best, and if given a chance, I'd gladly have a drink or two with them and reminisce about the old times.

Chapter 25:

Lincoln Center

After Lilly discovered me and brought me to the Ford agency, I had an interesting, if sporadic, career. Photographers loved to test with me – which is where they take practice shots and different techniques of lighting, backgrounds, etc. So, I would, unfortunately, frequently be at horse shows or at college. This didn't help my modeling career. Plus, many models have sugar daddies: men that like to have them on their arms, take them to clubs, and out to dinner, and such, dress them up and show them off.

I was not interested in a sugar daddy, which limited my resources as far as the ability to buy clothes and makeup and hair things, etc., but it was an interesting career. I worked with some great photographers – really great photographers.

I had worked with the assistant to Milton Green. Milton Green was a famous photographer and cinematographer and had been Marilyn Monroe's boyfriend. His assistant took one of my favorite pictures, where my knees are pulled up against my chest, and it's cropped in such a way that you can't see I'm actually wearing short shorts; it looks like I'm naked. But I have this inscrutable smile. This got shown to the editors of *Vogue*, and they loved it. So, they called me to interview several other high-fashion models and me.

I got the gig, which was a great gig. It was making a film with Milton Green because a famous designer was being put in the Fashion Hall of Fame. Her name was Bonnie Cashin, and she made beautiful clothes. In the film, we used all cashmere capes and hoods, clothing that she made that was just gorgeous. The film was taken on the beaches of Quogue, which is just below Southampton on Long Island and is a very upscale community. We all stayed – the editors, the assistants, etc. – everybody stayed at Charles Addams's House. Yes, that's the Charles Addams of *The Addams Family*, the famous New York cartoonist.

So, we stayed at his house, and we had a great time in a very convivial atmosphere, but then we had to get to work and do the filming. And we went out on the beach and the sand dunes, and we would change into different outfits. They would film us as we were running down the beach, etc. There were very tall dunes in Quogue, and I got the idea to get to the top of one of these dunes and run down it, twirling my cashmere cape and hood, until I got down to the shore and I just collapsed into a cashmere puddle on the beach. This became the end of the film. It was quite a good scene.

The film was shown at Lincoln Center in New York City. All of the fashion people were there. They numbered in the thousands – I don't know exactly how many. I could probably look up how many people Lincoln Center can hold in its auditorium.

I had to be on a runway they had built way out into the audience, where they would have me in my cashmere cape, huddled on the ground. As soon as the film ended, I had to run off the runway, twirling, as I had down the dune in the film, and I was terrified because, in those days, high fashion models did not do runway; there was none of this flying back and forth to Paris; the whole Fashion Week stuff hadn't yet developed.

So, I had to sit for forty-five minutes in a little puddle. Then I ran off the runway, twirling. I did not fall into the audience, which I was sure I would do. I successfully completed my mission!

The film was a big hit; everybody liked it. But my interest in modeling was waning. I did some more work, but it just didn't appeal to me that much.

I had an interesting modeling career. It was fairly sporadic due to my preferring to be in college or *really* preferring to be at the horse shows. So, I was less than the perfectly behaved model, but people that wanted me wanted *me*.

Photographers love to do what we call *test*, which is where they take more experimental things they're working on and take shots. Plus, we would get copies of those photographs.